27

By

Ryan Davis

ISBN No: 978-0-9574495-0-3

Published By Sidewinder Books 2012
Sidewinderbooks@hotmail.com
Copyright © Ryan Davis

"Nature rejoices in illusion. If a man destroys the power of illusion, either in himself or in others, she punishes him like the harshest tyrant."
– Goethe

For Liz and Mabel

Chapter 1

Fastening the corrugated tube securely to the exhaust pipe, Jim Vale walked it around to the driver's seat then fed it through the open window. Got in the car, shut the door, wound the window up as far as the tube would allow and listened to the rain crackling across the windscreen. From the Kenelm Hills he looked out to the smattering of stars that hung above the blobs of yellow light that marked out the town. Shivering, he snorted the rest of the speed.

He called Lulu. No reply.

He thought about calling his mum. It had been five years since Jim had come to the conclusion that silence made more sense to her than he did. When he realised he couldn't make her listen, he left Hamblington, a small Black Country village, for Birmingham to start a band with Gary. The shaping of noise, the sounds of words and the meaning of them crashing together, helped make life understandable, at least for a while.

'Snitches' had hit number one in the summer of 1999, but 'Tell Me Reasons', The Tyrants' last single, had flopped. The drinking had become a problem. He was two stone heavier. His teeth were piss-yellow. Eczema was spreading up his legs and across his stomach with the speed and ease of fire across a woodland floor. Now, it was the twenty-sixth of November and nearing the end of a millennium; for some people, it was going to be the end of the world. Jim Vale was making sure that it would be the end for him. At the age of twenty-seven, he knew that suicide was the only way to escape the person he'd become.

He turned over the ignition. Fumes spluttered into the car. The muscles in his neck contracted and he puked onto the passenger seat. Gritty smoke rose up around him, like unsettled dust, and quickly he felt it fill his lungs.

Lost in fog.

Gasping for breath.

A black velvet curtain of silence dropped down upon him.

Chapter 2

"His eyes are open."

Sunlight slanted like taut rope across the white room. A figure walked through the shafts, broke them up and came towards him. A head appeared close to Jim's face.

"Now, if you can hear me, we need to know your name?"

Jim opened his mouth and out drooled, "Jiiirm."

He tried to pull the oxygen mask away, but his hands shook. The man in front of him had a narrow face with a wide moustache and thinning hair swept over the top of his head. He grabbed Jim's arm and eased it with persuasive force back onto the bed.

"It's okay. We don't want the drip popping out now."

Jim's eyelids felt heavy.

"You are lucky, lucky, lucky…"

Now sitting on the bed, the man gave a closed-lipped smile and folded his fine brown hands slowly over his leg.

"In your blood we found traces of lead, alcohol and amphetamines. Even something that resembled cat litter." The sun lit up the scalp on the doctor's bowed head as he raised his eyebrows for an explanation.

Jim closed his eyes then felt a gentle tap on his cheek.

"Jim? That's all. Tell us later what happened. There's a pot of cream on your bedside table for those eczema sores on your legs and stomach, okay? Now, most importantly, it looks like you need to rest."

A young nurse rolled a box with a telephone mounted on it next to Jim's bedside table, pulled a pen out of her hair bun and asked him for his full name. He told her, then searched her eyes for any recognition – there was none. He watched her scribble 'James Brian Vale' on a form.

"This is to phone one of your loved ones, James." She

smiled. "You'll have to tell them that you'll be in here for at least another night."

Jim couldn't call his dad. He'd died of a heart attack fifteen years ago while singing 'Cracklin' Rosie' to his new wife in a pub on Broad Street in Birmingham city centre, clutching his chest and keeling over onto the table of drinks. At the time it had been two years since Robin Vale had left Jim and his mum to live with Sherry, one of the coin collectors from the Kidderminster branch of his small chain of amusement arcades.

The last time Jim had spoken to his mum he told her he'd been to lay some flowers against his dad's head stone. She'd slapped him across the face, then scribbled down a list of numbers and told him that they were the co-ordinates of his father's place in the spirit world.

The nurse was holding out the phone to him, twisting the wire impatiently.

"Thanks," he said, taking the receiver and watching her shuffle over to adjust the drip of the man in the corner who was moaning thinly.

He punched in Dimpy's mobile number.

"Dimp? It's me."

"Where the fuckin' hell are you? Where you been the last two days?"

Dimpy was The Tyrants' manager. Small, stocky and bald with yellow tombstone teeth. Jim had witnessed him hold a broken bottle neck to a promoter's twitching eye in Newcastle because he wouldn't pay the full fee for the gig they'd played that night. The promoter was twice Dimpy's height, but Dimpy came out the better of the two. His brutal approach to business had benefited them financially, but it meant he had no space in his heart for sentiment, and Jim was glad that Dimpy was fifty miles away in Nottingham.

"I'm in hospital. It's okay, I'm fine."

"Oh, that's good. *You're* fine…" The cockney twang sharpened the words into tiny daggers. "You really don't know what quantity of shit you've created, Jim. Where are you? What hospital?"

"Birmingham."

"Birmingham? What the hell you doing there? Hold on, it doesn't matter. You've put us, *me*, in very deep shit."

"What?"

"Deep, deep shit. Thanks to you and your little vanishing act we had to tell the booking agent you have exhaustion. So they've cancelled the rest of the French tour. And the whole of Europe – the *only* place in the world that looks like it gives a crap about you. Which means we owe *them* twenty grand. Gary's nose is, well… he'll need surgery to straighten that mess out. Got to say that was the weakest right hook I've ever seen, son. What did I tell you? I told you to get some help. Lay off the stuff for a while. But do you listen –"

"I couldn't take things going wrong anymore." Jim pushed his mouth into the phone and whispered, "I tried to top myself. Someone pulled me out of your car and dumped me at a hospital."

"It was you who stole it? You *stupid* bastard," Dimpy said.

The man in the bed next to Jim, who had both legs in plaster, was squinting, concentrating on Jim's conversation. Jim smiled at him and turned away to the window.

"In one sense I *do* want you to die at this moment in time," said Dimpy. "I ain't going to lie. But I won't fund it. You're under contract to *me* and you're losing a lot of people a lot of money. These stupid bloody stunts have gone on too long. Your vanishing act in Berlin? The night we cancelled in Amsterdam because you were too mashed to sing? In a way you've done me a huge favour. I can say it now, 'cause it's contractual. You're sacked, son."

Jim's stomach lurched like he'd just raced over the brow of a hill and the car had slammed down quickly on the other side.

"You can't do that! I'm –"

"I'm sorry, son. You're more trouble than you're worth and unless you can afford a good lawyer I suggest you shut the fuck –"

Dimpy went silent. Jim thought the phone might have cut off, but then he heard a radio, bouncy pop, somewhere in the background. He was just about to reply when Dimpy burst back on the line.

"Right. Your stupidity may have saved your bacon, boy. Listen to me or you won't even be able to *buy* a record let alone record one ever again. Do as I say: lay low until after New Year."

"Why?"

"Why? The press hasn't heard the new album yet – but I think with a tweak here and there it'll be bloody great. A missing singer is gold dust for a music paper. Is he dead? Isn't he dead? Has he gone to rehab? Or has he gone bloody nuts like Syd Barrett, living in a bedsit, washing in the same pot he pisses in? We release the album, and all the little girlies that bought 'Snitches' and made The Tyrants number one for a week in the summer may start to worry where you and your lardy arse have been for the last few months and buy it. All you have to do is pretend that you're dead. It's column inches. Death sells. After we make the cash back, you're out the band."

"I'm not dead yet. And you can't sack me." Jim felt his hand tightening around the phone, the pressure building in his throat. "*I'm* sacking *you*!"

"Ha, very funny! You're skint. I know that. The amount of shit you've gobbled up and drunk over the last year. You haven't got a leg to stand on, son. Check your contract. You broke it by leaving a tour and not reporting your whereabouts, *and* you've no other way of paying me back."

Jim felt like he'd been injected with a local anaesthetic; powerless.

"This is what'll happen. I line up a tour. Gary sings. We pay the agent off. In the New Year you tell the papers you've left The Tyrants, we get a new singer and you're free to do what you like. Drink yer 'ead off, I don't care. Until then you'll have nothing off me – 'cause you owe me and I own you. It's either that or we go to court. I'm doing you a huge favour. Just hope to fuckery that this works and gets some of those albums sold. Okay? Oh, and make sure Burt doesn't tell anybody or I'll slice his skinny knackers off."

Dimpy hung up.

Jim put the phone down. The nurse with the pen in her hair came over to him and said, "Just the one call? Is there anyone else?"

There was Lulu. He wanted to hear the music of her voice. Tell her how much he loved her. How much of a prick he had felt for what he'd done.

"No. That's it, thanks," he said.

The nurse rolled the phone away from the bed. Jim slid down under the starched white blanket, anger burning in his stomach. Not only had his final grand gesture, his last encore, been taken from him, but he had woken up in purgatory. He was neither dead nor alive, until he'd paid off Dimpy. What he should do was go to the press. Kick up a fuss, tell them exactly what Dimpy was doing. But he would need to hire a press agent to get any coverage and then – worst of all – it would look like he cared. No, he would do what Dimpy had said, vanish for a while. He'd put on weight, he'd cut off his long black hair with clippers and he'd begun to grow a beard. He hadn't been asked to sign an autograph for the last month. It wouldn't be hard for Jimmy Tyrant to disappear. He already had.

In the night he was woken by the moans of the old man with two broken legs. Jim pulled the pillow over his head.

He could remember now the thud that shook the car.

His head flicked up by a rasping cough.

Frantic knocking on the window.

A muffled voice.

A blast of cold air swooping into the car as he was pulled through the door and fell onto cool, wet mud.

Retching, his eyes half open.

"Mate…" A foot coming towards his head and nudging his shoulder. "You stupid bastard, you okay? Jesus, shit… Leanne, daft sod's tried to top himself…"

The suck and splash of feet running away.

The rain falling onto the mud sounding like applause.

An engine starting.

Then a bigger sound taking over, a melody he'd never heard

before twisting its way into existence somewhere inside him. He'd tried to grasp hold of it, follow the rush of magnificent sound coursing through him, but it kept tugging away. He knew he had to follow that music as it lurched down deeper and deeper, to a place of no light or standing, and the deeper he went, the weaker he became, but he held on tightly as it dragged him into the darkness, down, down, down, down, down...

The next morning Jim lay fully clothed on the bed waiting for the doctor to give him the all-clear. He picked up his smoke-sodden leather jacket and pulled out his notebook. Written in red ink across the back page was a phone number he'd been given after a gig in Paris last year while promoting their first album, *Here Come The Tyrants*.

For two years they'd toured the 'toilet circuit' of Britain in a converted ambulance. He'd witnessed big-boned drummer Paulo suck the flesh off a whole rotisserie chicken every meal-time for a month. He'd seen Gary, trousers around his ankles, arse pumping up and down, fucking girls on the seat next to him. He'd heard the bass player, Lonny, have many a wank. Bound by music and hope for a better life, The Tyrants had become the brothers he'd never had. But very quickly Gary, guitarist and Jim's song-writing partner, had got jealous of the attention Jim was receiving from the press, from the label, from girls, from just about everyone. When Gary found out that Finnish producer Bix Pillar had asked Jim, after the gig in Paris, whether he wanted to work with him on a solo project, the balance changed overnight. From then on Gary did everything he could to take control.

Jim ran his index finger up and around the dents in the paper that the numbers had made, the music he'd heard lying in the mud ringing in his head.

The A&E department was full, mostly of teenagers with burns from fireworks, and the doctor looked sweaty and flustered when he stood at the end of Jim's bed. It was clear he had neither the time nor the inclination to pursue the reason for Jim being there, and because Jim could walk and his results were fine, there was no need to keep him in. Jim gave the doctor a flat smile, stood up and shook his hand. He waved goodbye to the man with the broken legs and thanked the nurse with the hair bun for all her help. In the hospital shop he brought a small bunch of carnations, a box of Milk Tray, and made his way to the bus stop in the car park.

Chapter 3

After an hour-and-a-half journey on the bus, Jim arrived in Hamblington. He took the shortcut across the wet, cloudy fields, came out onto the road outside his old house and made his way up the garden path.

He rang the bell and after a moment Auntie Viv opened the front door. Fag in her mouth. Slim. Bleached hair in a ponytail. Almost identical to his mum before she stopped watching the TV and started using an Ouija Board to find out the next day's weather forecast.

Jim smiled. He waited for Viv to smile back, but she turned away, looking into the hallway.

"Quick, come in. Come on. You're letting the cold air in," she said, walking slowly into the lounge.

The house smelt the same: lavender, cigarettes and frying fat. Jim sat down at the dining table. Viv shuffled into the kitchen and came out with a cup and saucer. She placed them on a doily in front of him.

"Just brewed up a pot of tea." She sat down in the chair opposite him.

The sound of a carriage clock ticking filled the space between them as they sat in silence for a while, until Jim pushed the Milk Tray and carnations towards her.

"Merry Christmas," he said.

Viv regarded her gifts with a weak smile.

"Where's Mum?"

"Havin' a bit of a nap." She nodded towards the stairs. "So you had some spare time to see us then?"

Jim coughed into his hand and looked around the room. It had remained untouched since he'd left. A TV and video covered with a fine dust. A globe-shaped drinks cabinet, open, filled with whisky bottles: four empty and one full. By the kitchen door the carpet was worn down, exposing the lino, and a small, blue, plastic Christmas tree sat alone on the shelf above the two-bar fire. Sadness had descended and taken root deep within every object in the room, forbidding anything to be moved or be replaced.

"How's her ankle?"

"It's fine. She's out the wheelchair and walking like she's had an argument with a bus and lost, but…" Viv lit a cigarette. "You know how she is. I'm looking after her."

They caught each other's eye for a moment.

Viv picked up the box of chocolates and began to study the flavours.

It had been like this between them since Jim and his mother had moved in after his dad died. Vic had taken in her heartbroken sister and helped her the only way she knew how – to drink and talk it out, telling her that she had to forget Robin Vale and that her family was all she needed now. From then on Jim always felt that his very presence was interference in Auntie Viv's life and his mum's road to 'getting better'.

Viv looked at the end of her fag as she blew smoke out into the room. He could smell that she'd already had a drink.

"I've come because… because I want to help Mum out. You and Mum, out, I mean."

Viv, still looking at her cigarette, furrowed her brow and gave a ridiculing snort. "You don't need to, Jim. I'm doing everything the doctor said I had to. She gets her benefits. She's taking her tablets."

Jim looked to the globe and the empty bottles. "Do you think she should be taking pills and drinking, Viv? I thought you had it under control. She shouldn't be falling down the stairs and breaking her leg…"

Viv dropped her head back, her bloodshot eyes focusing on the large, yellow nicotine stain on the ceiling. He knew that from the start she'd never had it under control.

"Why now, Jim? It's been five years since you left. She doesn't need you. I know what's best for her, okay? I'm doing what the doctor said."

Feeling his chest tighten with anger, Jim stood up. He'd

never confronted Viv before and couldn't do it now. Not yet.

"Is she upstairs?" Jim said, making his way to the door.

"Yes. But she'll be asleep," Viv shouted after him.

Jim bounded up the steps in sets of two. He knocked on his mum's bedroom door and slowly pushed it open. A smell like fermenting apples and damp clothes rolled over him.

In the faint light coming through the curtains, above the plum-and-white squares of the knitted blanket, he could see the back of her head. Her once-blond hair was now slate grey. He noticed a chamber pot, full to the brim of brown piss, in front of her wardrobe. The pit of his stomach jumped to touch his throat.

He took a step closer and sat in the curve of her legs.

She still slept on her side of the bed. The blanket on his dad's side was flat and smooth, the pillow plump and untouched. The rest of the room was bare. Her dressing table, once covered in jewellery, perfume bottles and make-up, was clear, the mirror dull with a grainy film. No pictures on the walls. No photos on the shelves. Only an empty wine glass and a new collection of multi-coloured pills on a chair next to her bed. He picked up the glass and sniffed it; some brand of cheap whisky.

Jim gently tapped her arm, but she didn't stir. He held her shoulder and rocked her slightly.

"Mum?"

He dipped his head to listen. The bed covers smelt heavily of sweat and dead skin. Her breathing was deep and slow. With the concoction of those pills and drink she wouldn't be up for a while. God knew how long she'd been lying there, softening like fallen fruit.

He stood up slowly. She didn't stir. He looked back down at his father's side of the bed, a space that seemed frozen forever.

"Bye, Mum… I'll be back. I'm going to help you. I promise."

Jim waited for a moment, his shoulders tense in anticipation. He waited some more, staring at her mouth.

Nothing.

It was wrong to have left her back then, to never have called, but there was no other option. He wasn't wanted. He couldn't make himself heard and when he tried, no one listened. It was time now, he thought, to make things right.

"I should have done more… I promise I'm going to help you," he said.

Then he swallowed hard, left the room and ran down the stairs. Viv's eyes were closed. Her mouth gaped open and her cigarette still in her hand, rested on the table, streaming curls of smoke through the pale sunlight. Jim gently plucked it from her fingers and stubbed it out in the ashtray.

He closed the door quietly behind him and headed across the fields, back to Hamblington.

The phone box was next to the railway station. It was the same red box with smashed glass that had been there since he was a kid; the one in which he and Gary used to smoke a spliff when it was raining and dream of getting on the next train to anywhere, anywhere but here.

Jim picked up the receiver and dialled.

"Hey… Burt? Yeah, it's me, Jim. No, no, I'm back. Yes. About that money I owe you. Yes, I'm back. I'll be over this afternoon, yeah? We need to talk. I've got a proposition for you."

Chapter 4

Burt was as thin as electrical wire. His teeth were twisted brown shards. His hair, fine grains of black stubble, formed a faint triangle above his forehead. In an aqua-blue dressing gown, fag burns down the front, and with bare feet, he led Jim down the hallway of his dilapidated three-storey house just out of the city centre, in Balsall Heath,.

A dog was barking somewhere out the back. Toots and the Maytals on the stereo. The sweet-sour smell of marijuana and incinerated food.

Five years ago Burt had sold Jim and Gary whizz at a mod club. They had become regular customers, then friends, and quickly moved into Burt's house. Not long after that, to keep himself afloat between gigs, Jim began working with Burt, selling skunk and pills to a small network of promoters and musicians.

"You remember Stuart?" Burt pointed into a room on the left. A man with white dreadlocks and a ginger beard was lying, passed-out, open-mouthed and naked, amongst open pots of paint and torn-up sheets of canvas.

"No."

"You do. Fell asleep and shat himself in court."

"What was he up for?"

"Up for? He was training to be a junior barrister."

"Right..."

"Now, apart from getting high and talking new age hippy shit about the oneness of the universe, he paints. As you can see."

They walked down the hallway into the lounge. Sitting on the low sofa was a young woman with vinyl-black hair pulled up into a ponytail, wearing an oversized white leather jacket and grey tracksuit bottoms. She looked up as they entered, sucking her cheeks in as she pulled on her cigarette. No make-up. Wrecked pale-blue eyes.

"This is Nina. Nina, Jim."

Nina smiled at Jim coyly. She crossed her arms and rubbed her shoulders. "Hello Jim," she said dreamily and looked down at the ashtray. Next to it lay a mirror frosted with white powder.

"She's shy, aren't ya! She's Latvian, not much English… but we're sorting that out, hey, Neen!"

Nina sniffed and rubbed her eyes. "No, Burty… well maybe a little."

"Come on, son. Time to talk business."

Jim followed Burt into the kitchen, under a band of burnt toast and weed smoke, through a purple door, and into his office. Burt sat down behind a wooden desk littered with unused coin bags. In the centre was a pair of brass weighing scales. Jim sat in the chair opposite and looked out of the tiny window on his left. A pitbull terrier was chained up to a metal stake. It was barking and lurching towards the fence at the bottom of the yard.

"You haven't got a bag. You still haven't got the money for the batch of pills I gave ya for the tour, have ya?" Burt said, his black eyes wide in their sockets.

"Eh? Hold on, Burt. Where's the, 'How are you? How you doing? It's been a while?', and then I say, 'Well, no. Fucking awful actually.' You know, shit like that."

Burt leaned back from the table into his chair. He put an arm round the back of his head, nodded and pushed his bottom lip out.

"Oh, yeah. Peachy. The world is a fantastic place to live in and all that bollocks. But seriously. You ain't got the cash, have ya, mate?"

"I've got it, yeah. But it's going to take a bit of time. That's all. That's what I wanted to ask –"

"How long, Jim? Eh?"

"I've owed you money before and you've been fine."

"Jim. I know what's going on. It's different this time, innit?"

"Nothing's going on… What do you mean, different?"

"Your manager called me. Mr Dimpleton." Burt cocked his head, eyes arrogant. "He said he would cut ma' balls off if I told anyone about you being back in Brum. He also told me about you punching Gary in the face at the sound check in Nottingham. Running away. Pretending ya dead, are ya?"

Burt's gown had fallen open, showing his xylophone-like chest. He pulled over a tin box, opened it and began to roll a spliff. "He's not giving you any money, is he? He's frozen any money from The Tyrants' record sales going into your account."

"I've just got to clear a few things with him first, then it's all good. You'll get it."

"Clear twenty grand?"

"It's not all me. *I* don't owe twenty grand, not the exact amount, just part of that –"

"You're out the band, you owe a shitload and you ain't got jack, mate. That's the truth of the matter."

"Come on, man. You know I can get it. I helped you out in the past with deals. I got you all those support bands coming through town, all the tour crews. That's a lot of gear, man. A lot of pills. A lot of weed." Jim looked around the tiny room. "To be fair, since I left, I thought you would be doing better than this."

Burt peered up wearily from his tobacco tin. "I agree, you've helped me out. But I wouldn't say it equals staying at my house and never paying me rent for two years. I wouldn't say that it all adds up to a recording contract. Who was it that loaded up the A&R man from Olympic Records with a shitload of coke? After that stint in the bogs he came out shouting that you were going to be bigger than God's dick! You know, if it wasn't for me you'd still be singing to one man and his whippet in the Moseley Arms, being pushed off the stage so the punters can get at the faggots and peas."

"You may have noticed that I'm not exactly selling out Wembley at the moment."

"That's not my fault, mate, is it?"

Jim's whole body became rigid, inert with anger or defeat.

At that moment they felt like the same thing.

"You're stuck, mate. F.U.C.K.E.D.," Burt said softly, then popped the roll-up in his mouth and lit it.

"I do realise, okay? Look, you want contacts – more bands, label owners, producers, stuff like that. I can give you them. But I'm not going back to The Tyrants. Gary was trying to get me out of the band way before this. That's it. I'm going to make a solo record. And to make it with who I want and how I want means I need cash, man. I'm supposed to have vanished off the face of the earth, so I can't work in a pub or shop. We need to sort something out here, some type of agreement?"

The dog had stopped barking.

Burt chugged a deep one from his spliff and tapped a finger on his forehead. He studied Jim through undulating plumes of smoke, letting the silence build the pressure between them.

"Work for me. Like old times. Like when you and Gary first moved in, hustling for gigs, man, hustling for cash. Trying to stay alive."

"I worked *with* you. I want to be a partner."

"You can't afford to be a partner at the moment, not for what I'm dealing these days."

"Dealing?"

"Nah. You don't deal. You'll be dropping stuff off. You know, saving me a lot of hassle, like. I've taken on a lot more clients recently. And they're good clients now. It's not like when we first started, the odd bit of whizz here and there."

Jim hoped not. Once, in a pub car park in Winson Green, a young woman had refused to pay for the whizz she was going to take to her other half in the prison. She held a butter knife to Jim's throat as her baby looked on, sucking a toy car in its buggy. Jim handed the whizz over, not so much scared for his own life, but for hers and the baby, wondering what the hell would happen to her family if her husband didn't receive his stash.

"I don't know, Burt… For this stupid fuckin' stunt to work, to get the music press interested, to keep Dimpy happy and for me to get back to recording songs, I can't go wondering around town selling drugs to students. Most of them bought

'Snitches'. They'll know me. I'll need to be well hidden."

Burt stood up and sat on the desk in front of Jim.

"I do the bands, the venues. You do the more exclusive clients and stay away from that world… I wouldn't worry about anybody recognising you anyway."

"Hey, thanks, man."

"Nah, geez, nah. What I mean is a lot of my clients are businessmen now. Lawyers and doctors, like… Your beard's coming on nicely. I mean no offence, but 'Snitches' was a while back. You look a bit different from then, bit of a fat fucker now… Hey! Just kidding, mate. Trust me. Okay?"

Jim gave him the Vs.

"You want to sort your wardrobe out too. Dump the leather jacket and skinny jeans. You can't play at being Iggy Pop now. You need to blend in a bit more. I'll give you some of my old stuff." Burt grinned. "I'll sort you out. No one will know you from Adam, mate."

"Just till I pay you back?"

Burt's hand came down on Jim's shoulder. "We say three weeks for the payback money. Then, you need personal cash?"

"Big time."

"Ten per cent off all following deals. For your record fund."

Jim smiled. As long as he kept it low-key this would be the easiest and quickest escape route he could take.

"Where am I going to stay?"

"Well, Stuart has the front room. And if it all goes to plan, I should be having my girl move in soon."

"Nina's your girlfriend? You're joking?"

"Ah, only rock stars can get the good-looking ones? Fuck off, Jim. Dealing gets you girls, gets you money, and you don't have do all that travelling, pressing flesh and talking bullshit to journalists. You're way out of favour these days, kid. You couldn't pull a muscle."

"So what about the loft then?" Jim said.

"I'm turning the loft into an observatory for my telescope," Burt said, looking out of the window to the dog that was still straining towards the fence.

"Eh?"

"The stars, mate. Everyone needs a place to escape. Reach for the stars!" He threw a hand to the ceiling and flopped his head back. "Don't worry about accommodation; I can make you disappear. Put you up at this hotel in town I use for deals. You wouldn't know it was even there. The owner likes coke to impress his boyfriends. He'll let you stay there for a while then give you a discount rate or summat."

Burt grabbed the top of Jim's arms with a scrawny, tight grip. "This is going to be like the good old days!"

"In the centre of town, Burt?"

"Like I say, you'd hardly know it's there." Burt brought up the dog end of his spliff and sucked down a lungful of smoke.

"Like a black hole?"

"Like a what?" said Burt.

Chapter 5

Between a porn shop and an abandoned theatre, The Railway Hotel nestled like a group of neglected cells in the belly of Birmingham city centre.

He was now Robbie Johnson, a name he'd adopted to check in to hotels on tour. His beard was full, his head completely shaved and he was dressed in Burt's cast-offs: an 'I Ran the World' t-shirt, combat trousers and a green Puffa jacket. Walking past the Chinese restaurants and pool halls, his reflection in the front windows was that of a young Hell's Angel at a rave.

In the hotel reception four men with cropped hair and thick necks sat in cigarette-smoke-filled shafts of sunlight watching horse racing on a TV chained to the wall. The man behind the desk was tall and skinny and had chestnut-brown skin. He wore a navy-blue blazer with gold buttons. Under it an ice-white shirt unbuttoned one too many revealed where his tan stopped.

"I don't know if Burt contacted you?" Jim asked.

The man opened up the diary on the desk in front of him, and ran a long, thin finger down what was clearly a blank page. "Ah yes. Room nineteen. Twenty quid a night without breakfast. Twenty-two, with. It's at the top so you've got your own bathroom. You can bring back who you like, just leave the room clean and tidy. Robbie Johnson?"

"Robbie Johnson, yeah. I haven't got my passport, I'm afraid."

"Hum?" The man looked at him inquisitively.

"My ID."

The man stared at him blankly for a moment, then wrote 'Robbie' on a cardboard fob. He attached the fob to a key, and handed it to Jim.

"Just follow the stairs as far as they go." He looked up, gave a flat smile and raised a stagey eyebrow. "The Penthouse."

Signed pictures of The Krankies, Canon and Ball, Duncan Norvelle and other faded stars of light entertainment adorned the walls of the five flights of stairs that Jim had to climb to get to what, in reality, was the attic. The wallpaper in the room was yellow with clusters of large, pale-pink roses. A portable TV with a coat hanger for an aerial sat on a table at the end of the bed. There was a small window looking onto the street and the back of the train station. The room to the left contained a pink plastic bath with a faint grey line running halfway up around the inside. As he sat on the bed he noticed a large dark stain on the brown carpet and tried not to imagine what could have made it. Jim propped himself against the headboard, pulled his feet up and closed his eyes.

In the last year he'd stayed in Holiday Inns and found some comfort in their bland consistency. It was while at a Holiday Inn, during the final days of promoting their last single, 'Tell Me Reasons', to half-empty halls across Europe, that he'd received the news from Dimpy that his mum had fallen down the stairs and broken her ankle. Jim began a three-day drinking session that started in Holland. After the gig in a half-empty club in Amsterdam, during which he forgot most of the words and fell off the stage, they drove overnight to Berlin. The next day he found that his whisky had been taken, so he left the bus and went to find an off-licence. The following morning he woke up on a warehouse floor covered in sleeping punks with a crudely scrawled 'X' tattooed in green ink on the inside of his right forearm and a black love bite on his neck. He'd missed the previous night's gig, and on the bus journey to Calais the whole of the band blanked him. In his cabin on the ferry, and then on the bus to the gig in Nottingham, he drank uncaringly.

At the sound check, when Gary asked the engineer to turn Jim's vocals down on stage for the sixth time that tour, Jim found himself throwing down the mic, running across the stage, raising his arm and punching Gary in the face so hard that it knocked him to the floor.

The room was silent for a second.

Gary lay still, eyes closed. His guitar stared to feedback, the metal hum building.

Jim felt as if he had been woken abruptly from a dream: shaky and cold. With his knuckles stinging and the guitar wailing, he ran off stage, out of the venue, and that night slept rough under a railway arch.

The next morning Jim went back and stole Dimpy's car. He drove to the Kenelm Hills in Hamblington, full of disgust at his actions, unable to understand how it had come to this, and decided that it was time, once and for all, to stop causing so much trouble, for himself and everyone around him.

When he woke it was dark and the hotel sign was glowing orange outside his window. It would normally have taken him an hour to get ready: shampoo, mousse, blow-dry, tease, hairspray; matching shoes and belt; some black eyeliner that Lulu had given him. But there was no mirror or hairdryer in this hotel. In the room, by himself, he was James Vale again. A fat, shaven-headed James Vale with yellow eyes and fingers, fucked teeth and a thick black beard. He threw on the pair of combat trousers, the faded T-shirt and the comical-looking, over-sized jacket. He was now someone else: Robbie Johnson, drug dealer. Looking in the small mirror above the sink, he felt instantly more comfortable.

As he walked down the stairs the sound of the hotel bar rushed up around him. There was a small, low stage flanked by two speakers propped up on stools. Around the pool table six young lads dressed in tracksuit tops and jeans threw punches at each other's arms, laughing.

Jim sat on a stool at the corner of the bar. The smell of beer made him feel nauseous so he ordered a coke, then felt a tap on his shoulder.

"A swimmer, are you?"

It was the tall, chestnut-tanned man from reception that morning.

"Er… no," said Jim.

Jim saw a face that time and drink had pinched; now only charm and skin cream was holding it in place.

"It's the bald head. Like that swimmer chap… Goodhew. Duncan Goodhew!"

Jim laughed along with him. The man stopped laughing abruptly and held out his hand. His nails were long and perfectly manicured, his breath fruity.

"Tony."

"Oh, right, yeah. I'm working for Burt."

"Yes. Good lad, Burt. Okay now, is he?" He looked concerned.

Jim frowned at the question.

Tony flashed a big grin and said, "Oh, you know, ups and downs. Deals with a lot of bands. They're not paying as much as they used to. Showbiz is a fickle mistress."

Jim smiled. "I'm sure she is."

"We're having karaoke later. You see the lovely Dennis over there, with that group of chaps?" He pointed to one of the men by the pool table: twenty-ish, freckle-faced, a white Nike jumper, a tramline shaved into the side of his blond-highlighted hair, balancing a beer mat on his chin. "Got the voice of an angel. I'm helping him out in the business. He's going to be a star one day. So, shall I book you a place?"

Jim drained his glass. "I've got other plans tonight. Maybe next time."

"Ah, training at the pool, I completely understand. Next time!" Tony shouted after Jim as he walked towards the door.

Burt had told him that Lulu was playing requests at The Champagne Bar on Fridays. Every other Sunday she was at a lesbian bar called The Chain Makers, playing piano for a woman called Gee-Gee as she sang songs from pre-war Berlin. Before he went to The Chain Makers he had to find a quiet place to make a phone call, so he walked to Digbeth and into The Royal George. He wanted a whisky but ordered an orange juice. Pulp's 'Disco 2000' fizzed from the speakers. Next to him sat a squat man with a white, wavy side-parting. His dry, stubby hand cupped a whisky. He was speaking to the barman and anyone who would listen.

"The bug! The Millennium Bug! All yer computers, yer fancy bollocks. Gone! Planes fallin' from the sky. From the *fucking* sky! Hospital machinery running into the ground! Dead bodies all over! And the banks: money flying out of the holes in the wall!" The old man spun right round and fixed Jim with a glassy stare. "It's fucking Armageddon! Sell yer soul just to live. All will change. It's the end for ya!"

The barman rolled his eyes.

Jim smiled warily and walked into the quiet of the empty back room and sat down. He pulled out his notebook and the phone Burt had given him. He flicked it to the last page, where he'd written Bix Pillar's number. He looked over the sagging loops of the sixes and eights, the curved ones that may be sevens and the sloping numbers between; were they threes or fives? It was a number scrawled drunkenly and in haste. Had Bix just been music-industry bullshitting? Was he telling Jim how great he was so that if Jim actually did have a hit, Bix could say that after a gig in a half-empty strip club in Paris, he was one of the privileged few who spotted that Jim's genius was too big for The Tyrants to contain? Jim didn't even know what time was it in Finland.

Fuck it. He could always leave a message.

He dialled and waited.

"'Lo?" The clamour of feedback swirled down the line.

"Bix?"

"'Lo?" Feedback and screaming voices.

"Bix? It's Jim Vale. Jimmy Tyrant?" Jim said louder.

"Yah. Wait." The screams and feedback faded and he heard a door slam.

"Shoot."

"Hi, Bix, it's Jimmy Tyrant, from The Tyrants. You talked with me in Paris about us doing an album together. You said I reminded you of Iggy Pop. Said you thought my lyrics were up there with Lou Reed's?"

"Ah… Paris? Jim. The Tyrants, yes! It's been a while. You are okay?"

"Yeah, well. Sort of. It's complicated… I'm calling about

what you said, about the solo album. I've got some songs that I wanna put together and I'm basically saying, yes, I'll take you up on the offer, do a solo album. The sooner the better."

"Ha, yes. Well. Okay... if only you had called, like two days before..."

"Oh, why's that?"

"I've just taken on a very big project. Secret? But let me say one word: Björk."

"Björk. That's great. I always thought you two should make a record..."

"Yeah, well. Perfect. She wants me to record a herd of polar bears giving birth on the strike of the Millennium. It's always one on one with Bix. And it's Björk so... Listen, you are pretty well unknown all over – I heard your last single. The hip-hop beats over a garage rock song, what were you thinking?"

"Bix, please don't judge me on that. After 'Snitches' went to number one the label thought it was the best way to get another hit. It had nothing to do with me, I assure you."

"Look, I have to say, you are a liability. But you have something, er, raw. Unknown. I like your voice, your act, Jimmy. But it will take me to make you a star. Okay? I'm not working New Year's Day. Forget it, but after I have two weeks free. From the fifth of January."

"That sounds great." Jim's heart was hammering against his shirt – that was two weeks before his twenty-eighth birthday.

"Two things. Bring songs. And bring money. For you? Ten thousand. I'll make the best album for you. Okay?"

Down the line Jim heard a door clunk open; feedback squealing again.

"I have to go. Bye-bye." Bix hung up.

Jim's head felt light, and his body numb. If Burt was dealing what he said he was dealing then it shouldn't be a problem, especially with all the Millennium parties. Jim had just over a month to get the cash and get some songs together. He had the lyrics, he just needed the music.

The Silk Cut clock behind the bar said 00.10.

He downed his drink and left.

A heavy-set bouncer stood in the doorway of The Chain

Makers, her ash-blond hair scraped back, feet touching the side of the entrance. She shook her head from side to side even before he spoke.

"Sorry, mate."

"What, 'cause I'm a man?"

"No. 'Cause you look like shit. There's a themed dress code, like. And you're nowhere near it."

"I've come to see Louise –"

"There's loads of 'em in there, pal." She sniffed and looked over his head.

"No… I know. Louise is the pianist for Gee-Gee?"

"Is she?"

"Yeah. So, I just want to –"

"You're not going in on any level."

She folded her hands over her crotch and looked up the road as if he had already left.

Jim walked around the back and looked through a window. The stage was empty. Lulu must have been on her break.

He found the stage door and knocked. Nothing. He knocked again and waited, and then heard faint footsteps from behind the door. As they got louder, he felt his stomach pinch; his testicles and arse become slick with sweat. The door opened. Lulu stood in the frame, her black hair, shining under the lamplight, pulled back into a ponytail. She was wearing a dinner jacket with a pink buttonhole and white silk culottes. Her lips were blood-red and her eyelids a smoky grey. She wrapped her arms round herself and squinted to see him.

"I'm back on in five. If this is anything to do with another cruise ship deal, I'll tell you now –"

Jim pulled out of the shadows of the door and stood with a big smile under the street lamp in front of her.

"Hi, Lu."

Her eyes narrowed. "My God…" Then she turned quickly and ran back into the club. Jim rushed towards her, but the door closed fast in his face and he was left in the orange scent of her wake.

He banged a few times. The door flew open and he was greeted by the sarcastic grin of the bouncer.

"You again?"

She went to grab his arm. Jim twisted himself away and threw up his hands in defence.

"Okay. Okay. Fine. I'm walking, walking back to the street. Okay?"

He wandered back up into town. The Bull Ring shopping centre had been demolished since he'd left the city a year ago to go on tour to promote *Here Come The Tyrants*. He walked up to the fence that surrounded the hole where it once stood, slipped his fingers through icy metal mesh and peered down. A huge black mouth looked back at him, the building joists snapped and exposed like rotten teeth. The Shipwreck Club had been levelled to the ground too. Memories of The Tyrants' first gig there – his hands shaking ecstatically on the mic stand before the first song – flashed through Jim's head. He experienced a strange feeling, like joy, loss and sadness were converging all at once. The sensation was too big, too painful to make sense of, so he turned and strode quickly up the street, back to the hotel, with the image of Lulu's face in the lamplight fixed like a frame from a movie in his mind.

Jim leaned against the bar of The Railway Hotel, above which hung pink-sequined banners that said *2000! Millennium!* He watched a procession of pissed and rambling renditions of karaoke classics by the locals. Then Dennis, the beer matt balancer Tony had pointed out earlier, grabbed the mic, stood with his eyes closed, legs apart, and waited for the music to begin. A couple of giggling women seated down the front waved their hands slowly above their heads to the intro music. He sang 'Somewhere Out There' in a high, R&B-tinged voice, walking across the tiny stage and reaching out his hand to the front row. The lads at the snooker table looked on, respectfully bobbing their heads, beer held on their chests.

As the song ended, Dennis held the mic between both hands in a praying position. He slowly lowered them to his chest and stared meaningfully over the heads of the crowd, to the back of the bar. The room erupted into cheers. Dennis's face cracked with a large smile and he hopped off the stage.

His mates slapped him on the back.

Jim found himself shaking his head – he couldn't believe they were lapping up that sentimental crap from a boy with a fake American accent dressed in sportswear and wearing a bum-bag.

"Hey… Mr Johnson!" Tony waved Jim over.

A beer waiting for him, Dennis fell into the seat next to Tony, grinning and chewing gum open-mouthed.

Jim walked over.

"Sit down, sit down," Tony said.

A scrawny-faced man in a tweed jacket and tracksuit bottoms shimmied down the red leatherette seat. Jim slumped onto it. Tony's hand shot up and gestured with three fingers to the barmaid.

"Good swim?"

"Pool was being drained." Jim shrugged with a grin.

"Ha! Shame, shame."

Tony eased back. His yellow-tinged eyes swooped around the table and landed back on Jim, then he leant in towards him.

"I know who you are, sir."

"Duncan Goodhew. I understood who you were talking about, the bald swimmer from the eighties." Jim laughed and looked at the other men around the table, their faces haughty and flushed.

"Dennis told me. He recognised you."

"Eh?" Jim cocked his head.

"You're Jimmy Tyrant, from The Tyrants. 'Snitches.' Number one, wasn't it?"

"Who?" Jim looked baffled.

Tony moved back into the seat and moved in closer to Dennis, who was still chewing and smiling.

"Come on. Dennis saw you walk in earlier. He told me who you were the moment you left. A very keen eye this lad, ah?"

Tony placed a hand gently on Dennis's arm, but Dennis quickly flicked it off. Smile strained, Tony retracted his hand immediately.

"I thought, is that 'im? And I didn't say anythin', like. Know what I mean? But then I thought, I'll 'ave a closer look, and then, fuck me! It is! 'Snitches.' Good tune."

"So what did you think of him, *Mr Rock Star*?" Tony said.

Jim cleared his throat. "It's, well, it's not my thing, but, yeah, you can sing. No doubt about that..."

"I'm good. I know I am, mate. The people here fucking love me. The old women, the lads, the young girls. All across the board. You've got contacts. You could get me a showcase with a label, couldn't ya?"

The barmaid put a whisky in front of Jim. She placed one in front of Tony and gave another to Dennis.

"Well, it's difficult. It's very competitive these days. I'm not sure…"

Dennis stopped chewing and looked at him seriously.

"It'd be worth your while," Dennis said.

"What do you mean, worth my while?"

Dennis tore off a match.

"I saw the papers."

Jim picked up his glass, knocked the whisky back in one and placed it down on the table.

"Gone missing. You're officially missing, aren't ya?" Dennis looked around the table at the others and lit a cigarette.

Dimpy had been quick off the mark; the story was *already* in *Weekly Music Express*.

"It's not like that really… I just needed a break. I don't want to be hassled at the moment. That's all. Don't believe everything you read in the music press. It's just a story."

"Well, whatever, like, the stay here will be a lot nicer. And you won't get found…" He dragged on his fag. "Know what I mean?"

"Eh?"

"We. Won't. Tell. That's what you want, isn't it?"

Dennis clamped the fag tightly into the corner of his mouth, leant sideways, pulled out a CD from his bum-bag and pushed it across the table. He started chewing again, blowing out smoke. No smile this time. He concentrated on Jim's hand around the empty shot glass.

"I suppose fingers are important for musicians, eh? Strumming yer guitar or plonking yer piano…"

Jim set his hand on his lap.

"Be a shame for you to never be able to play an instrument again. Wouldn't it, mate." Dennis flashed a hard, squared-toothed smile.

"Okay… No problem. Yeah, fine. I'll try and get my A&R man at the record label to have a listen. No problem," Jim said, his face aching from the big grin he was pulling.

"Good choice. As I said, it'll be worth your while doing this, mate." Dennis winked and stubbed out his cigarette.

Jim nodded.

He finished off his pint, said goodnight to everyone at the table and made his way up the five flights of stairs to his room, his trembling hand clawing at the sores at the top of his thighs.

*

The next morning, Burt gave Jim the keys to an eighties-model, pastel-blue Escort and a list of drops for all over the city.

Two chefs at the Samson Hotel, on double shifts, wanted a stash of speed – they left a freezer bag containing the money under a large metal bin full of decomposing meat and veg.

The head of a software company whom Burt had got talking to at a party sent his personal assistant to fetch a bag of pills. Jim met her in a car park on a business estate in Solihull. She slipped into the passenger seat, her eyes nervously scanning the car for hidden cameras or listening devices. She threw a wad of cash on his lap, took the pills off the dashboard and, getting out, said, "It's all there," before walked off quickly, head down, across the tarmac.

There was a blond, tanned Reiki healer at a health spa in Sutton who wanted a block of Red Seal cannabis resin. A flat-faced Spanish man in a crumpled suit on Hagley Road had a four-ounce bag of coke and put an order in for the same in smack. And a wheelchair-bound old woman in a huge Victorian house in Edgbaston had a bag of skunk – for her

31

arthritis.

That first week Jim ate what he wanted and when he wanted. His body was no longer on show, no longer selling a product. The fatter he got, the more distorted the image of Jimmy Tyrant became. He was getting closer to how he imagined Robbie Johnson to be, getting closer to being someone else.

The car had a radio, but he didn't use it. He sang out his lyrics and tried out melodies to see which fit them best.

On the Friday afternoon he called up the council and organised for someone to assess his mum and Viv's living conditions. He called the Citizens Advice Bureau, who set him up with a contact number for a drugs and alcohol counsellor, then he trawled the Yellow Pages for private carers, jotting down their numbers.

Every evening he went back to the hotel and tried not to drink, but he had run out of the prescription painkillers for the sores on his legs; only whisky did the job. He avoided talking to people – when he was drunk he was likely to blab the whole stunt to anyone who would listen.

He watched the local news play out silently from the TV: Rackham's windows crammed full of gold-and-silver present boxes. Long queues of people waiting for the start of a sale. A sad-faced woman with a bank statement. Christmas trees being shoved into the back of Volvos. Christmas illuminations on New Street. A stage being erected in Centenary Square. A pint being squirted into a glass. Two women fighting outside a club on Broad Street in Santa hats. Banks of computers, mountains of grain, businessmen with grimaces watching stock figures. A clock ticking down to midnight.

The Railway Hotel floated outside all of that; just outside the world. These problems and events on TV weren't going to affect him. He drank and felt his limbs loosen, his brain slow down and thicken. He was lost and invisible, along with all the other men and women who ate, drank, sang and slept there. As long as the money was coming in, he didn't care, because for now invisible was just what he needed to be.

Chapter 6

"All this rest ain't doing you any favours, son! Look at his eyes, babe!"

Burt was right: Jim felt like crap. It was the fifth of December, one week since he'd started working for Burt, and he'd had a good run on sales. The record fund and cash for his mum had been piling up, and with any extra money he'd eaten out and then drunk whisky at the hotel bar.

"You look like shit, Jim," Nina said through closed teeth. She rubbed her nose with the back of her hand, then sniffed. She was dressed in a tight, neon-pink mini-skirt and boob tube. Her figure was skinny, with full breasts. When she finished the last line of powder on the table, Nina leant over, brought Burt's face to hers, gave him a forceful, open-mouthed kiss and sniffed. She stood in front of the mirror, fixed her glossy hair that tapered to a point at the base of her spine, threw on her jacket in a one smooth movement and strode out into the hallway.

Burt looked on, mouth open.

"See you later, baby," she said and slammed the door behind her.

"She's unbelievable, isn't she?" Burt said.

"She going clubbing?"

"Ha. Nah, geez, she's a dancer. Well… a stripper, like. At a place called Jumps. You know that Birmingham now has more strip clubs per square mile than Las Vegas?"

"Seriously?"

"Things have changed since you've been gone, son. Now all the industry has left, the place is getting a new image. It's all about clubs and shopping these days. They want you to spend money rather than make it! About time, if you ask me. She wouldn't be able to work anywhere else. Nina's an illegal. She

33

really wants to dance in musicals…"

"She loves you for your charm and boyish good looks, I take it," Jim said, looking down at the open bag of cocaine on the table.

"We both get what we want out of this relationship. I'm helping her out, she's helping me out."

Adjusting his balls, Burt stood and walked out into the kitchen. Cupboards slammed and cutlery chimed in drawers.

"Hey…" Jim shouted, leaning towards the open door,

"Tony knows who I am."

The banging stopped.

"Eh? What's that?"

"Apparently, this bloke called Dennis recognised me. He doesn't really look the type to read the music press."

Burt came in holding a coconut in each hand, green straws poking out the top. He had a white plastic shopping bag dangling from his arm. He put the drinks on the table and sat down.

"Dennis gave me a CD. Told me it would be worth my while getting him a showcase for my record label. He said if I didn't, he'd break my fingers, man… I saw him at the karaoke. Bloody awful."

"He won't touch you… I heard he was a good singer. Just flatter 'im. You'll be out of there in a few weeks."

Burt pointed at Jim's coconut, picked up his, threw out the straw and took a large swig. "Ah!" he gulped, eyes popping open. "Let's start earning that recording fee then. I've got a drop at this bloke's house. Just moved into your neck of the woods. You're from Hamblington, aren't ya?"

"I'm sure I won't be going to the council estate I grew up on…"

"Nah. The posh, countryside part. I can't go; I got some other stuff to work out."

Jim sucked up a mouthful of toxic-tasting milk liqueur, swallowed begrudgingly and nodded.

"Here you are then," Burt said. He put his coconut down and placed the shopping bag in front of Jim. Jim opened it and looked in.

"Someone having a party?"

*

Jim kept his eyes firmly on the road as he passed his old council estate. When the house was seized by creditors they'd moved from Bearwood to Hamblington, to live with Auntie Viv. A month after the move, his mother ran out of an expensive restaurant she used to visit with his father. Refusing to pay the bill, explaining she had a tab and the cost would be covered by the amusement arcade millionaire Robin Vale, she was arrested. She was let off with a caution and eventually diagnosed with manic depression. The doctor said that she'd probably always had it in some form, but this bout had been brought on by her excessive alcohol consumption. She was advised to take anti-depressants and to stop drinking. Jim would plead with her each morning to take her medicine and when she was in the bath he would find new places to hide her whisky bottle. But her stubbornness prevented her from taking the pills and she always found the bottle, or Viv would buy her another.

On those lonely nights, before he met Gary, Jim had listened to his dad's records in the dark of his bedroom. He talked to him as if he were there, about Lennon's scream on 'Twist and Shout', about the fierceness of the guitar solo on 'Sympathy for the Devil'. From then on his dad's music was his music. He dressed only in charity shop clothes and listened to nothing from after 1969.

Whistling 'Pink Moon' by Nick Drake, Jim drove onto a lane that ran out through wet, open fields. Behind loomed the hills, treetops draped in mist, where only a week before he'd tried to take his life. Pulling up outside large, black metal gates, he buzzed the intercom. The gates opened on to a tarmac road that disappeared into a pine wood. Jim followed it and shortly found himself in front of a three-storey, mock-Georgian house surrounded by a white gravel drive. A glass dome was attached to the end of the right wing, and on the left what looked like a huge silver corkscrew – a sculpture of some sort, Jim thought – poked incongruously into the sky.

Jim pressed the doorbell.

The door opened more quickly than he expected.

"Burt's lackey?"

Jim just about recognised Jacob Little, dressed in a black Wu-Tang Clan T-shirt, gold and diamond chains and pink Bermuda shorts. Four years ago his picture had featured on the front cover of every national newspaper. He'd become famous for selling his computer games company to a huge American conglomerate for one hundred and sixty million pounds. He was sixteen. He'd created the computer game character MaX Fist, a renegade commando who, disillusioned with the army, set up a team of mercenaries to take justice into his own hands. Jacob Little hadn't created a new game since. These days when his name was in print it was in articles complaining of music blasting long into the night from his extravagant and seemingly endless parties.

"Well, if you put it like that…" Jim said.

Jacob turned and walked into the hallway. His black flip-flops smacked across the white marble and a plump toiletries bag swung loosely from his hand.

"You got everything? Everything I ordered?" he said over his shoulder.

Jim followed him, eyeing the bizarre mural above his head.

"Yeah… What's going on with the ceiling?"

Jacob turned grumpily.

"It's a re-creation of the Sistine Chapel, but instead of angels and cherubs and all that shit, it's depicting the story lines from the games I created. See that section above the stairs?"

He pointed to the ceiling over the double-sided marble staircase – a muscular Jacob, long, flowing hair, a bolt of blue lightning between his hand and the hand of an even more muscle-bound man with a crew cut, dressed in combat gear, his teeth bared, mouth twisted, distorting the scar down his face.

"That's me giving life to MaX Fist. You know MaX Fist?"

"I'm not a gamer, but everyone knows MaX Fist."

"I invented him… But you knew that."

"Well, I've never played it."

"Thank God. I have all strains of shit coming here wanting to know about the next game… giving me tips." He turned and carried on walking.

Jim followed him into a long white sitting room. On his left was a fish tank that glowed blue, dotted with electric red and yellow tropical fish. Remote-control cars and games consoles lay toppled randomly over the carpet. Next to the long red-leather sofa a stack of empty, unwashed, frozen-meal cartons was piled as high as the armrest. The room smelt of dope, cold gravy and cabbage.

"Do you like hip-hop?"

Before Jim could answer, Jacob had taken a wafer-sized pad from his pocket and pushed a button. A glass panel descended from the ceiling.

"I love it," Jacob said flatly as a cheap-looking video for a hip-hop crew blasted across the glass and lit up the room.

"Who's that?"

Jacob stopped dead and turned, then gave Jim a look of contempt for his ignorance.

"The Krayzz? The best fuckin' hip-hop crew in Brum. You've never heard of them? Seriously?"

Jim looked up at the screen. "Oh, The Krayzz, right." He had seen large fly posters for their gigs on boarded-up buildings in Aston and Handsworth.

"Look at this," Jacob said.

Jim followed him through a frosted glass door. Jacob flicked a light switch to reveal a low-lit office. In the centre was a small desk with a mixer on top of a sleek new sound system. The back wall was lined with vinyl records and the other walls were covered in tatty-looking pink-and-green posters of The Krayzz. One was still attached to the plywood, taken from the window it had been protecting .

Jacob sniffed and nodded proudly at his collection.

"You really are a fan."

"I've got every poster The Krayzz ever made. And record. All white label, man. These boys spit the truth, you get me? True originators. Enough…"

Jacob switched off the light and they left the room and entered the glass-domed structure that Jim had seen from outside. The floor was covered in white studded leather. In the centre was a large brass telescope, angled to the sky. Attached to the side of it was a black leather chair.

"Flop where you like."

They sat opposite each other on the soft floor. Jim took the bag out of his Puffa jacket and placed in front of Jacob.

"Burt wants one of these," Jim said, pointing to the telescope.

"Yeah… He wants everything I've got." Jacob picked up the bag and sniffed it.

"Okay. You first, player."

He placed the open bag back in front of Jim and looked at him moodily with his head on his shoulder.

"It's a bit early for me," Jim said with a smile, looking round and admiring the room.

"That's the deal, kid." The word 'kid' conveyed a slight American accent. "That's why I used Burt the last couple of times. I trust him. But I don't know you."

Jacob pulled a silver handgun out of his pocket and placed it next to his leg. It was comically large with a square barrel. Jim tried to retain the same expression as before the gun was pulled. That's his game, he thought; the guns, the music – he sees himself as some kind of gangster rapper.

Jacob gave Jim a sarcastic smile and then looked down at the bag. "You could have swapped it for any old shit."

Jim held his gaze for a moment. "If you insist."

Jacob pulled down the loose neck of his T-shirt, showing his white, hairless chest, and took a small gold shovel off a chain and handed it to Jim. Jim scooped out a slice and snorted it. His eyes watered. He dropped his head back and sniffed hard.

Jacob stared at him, waiting for some reaction, searching Jim's eyes. "Look up," he said, and he peered up Jim's nose.

"Okay," Jacob said.

Lights exploded in Jim's head; his arms felt strong; a wasps' nest had broken open in his chest. "It's good shit," he said.

"I just don't want it to be poisoned good shit. You don't want to know the number of people who'd love to see me dead. For real."

Jim wanted to laugh at this kid. He really did think he was a gangster; he thought he was Ice-T.

"Who'd want you dead?"

"Are you serious? I couldn't even begin to tell you." Jacob snatched back the shovel and snorted some himself.

"Known Burt long?" Jim said.

"No. My old dealers were getting expensive and there were a few… er…" He pinched his nose and rubbed it vigorously. "… problems, internally. In their setup."

"Right."

Jim didn't want to know any more. He just wanted to leave. He'd had to stop himself taking any coke when he was at Burt's. He had that hot pull again – strapped to a rocket surging up from the world into a welcoming blue sky and on towards the stars. But now he was running out of fuel and plummeting fast, back down towards the hard earth. He swallowed and drove the nails of his left hand into the sores on the back of his right.

"Have you paid Burt yet?" Jim said quickly.

Jacob gave a lazy shake of his head, sucked his teeth and said in a street voice, "Bwaoy, wants to get a fucking grip of bidness, you get me." He unzipped the toiletries bag. It was stuffed full of fifty- and twenty-pound notes. He reached in and pulled out a handful and threw them down on the floor in front of Jim.

"Count it out in front of me."

"So when's the new game out?" Jim said, picking up the scattered notes.

The Wu-Tang Clan's 'C.R.E.A.M.' played out loudly from the speakers Jacob lay on his back, singing along. After the first chorus Jacob stopped the track, rolled over onto his stomach and looked up at Jim with wide, unfocused eyes.

"I'm taking my time. It's hard for you to understand. I'm not sure if you have any dreams, ambitions. No offence, it looks like you don't… You see, I thought up this world. MaX

Fist's world, right? He was everything a skinny kid, fat kid, crippled kid, freaky kid with no friends wants to be. In my world you take on the bad guy and you can win… It just went massive and sold, like, shitloads. So I bought this house, packed Mum and Dad off to the south of France and bought everything I ever wanted." He coughed and looked confused.

"You've got a new game coming out then?" said Jim pointedly.

For a second Jim saw the face of a twenty-year-old – uncertain, searching, open. Then, as soon as it came, it vanished – back to that of a man who had seen too much.

"I'm an artist. A manipulator of other realities. It came easily when I was younger. What *I* did was sell my universe to the rest of the world. Now I'm left trying to make the real world like the one I sold. That's what the shrink told me anyway."

Jim nodded. "Yeah… I know what you mean."

"You haven't got a fuckin' clue, kid. Not a clue. Yer man, Phaser from The Krayzz, the whole of The Krayzz. Now there's a man and crew that never sold out. Done everything they could to keep it real. Keep it gangster, man. They get respect!" Jacob shouted.

He lifted another spoonful of the gold shovel to his nose, sniffed and turned to Jim, his mouth twisted into a grimace. "Is Burt okay? He was a little distracted when he came here last."

Jim nodded quickly.

"Good, he's okay! Is he coming to the Millennium party?"

"Millennium party?"

"My Millennium party. Do you think all this stuff is for me!" Jacob laughed cruelly. "Well, we've got to get through Christmas, yeah, but it's all part of the run-up to the Millennium. I'm starting to cut down the wood out the back, and I'll have a huge bonfire, fireworks, thousands of people. A massive free party, free stylin', bands, DJs. In the new year, I wanna build a fairground on the land."

Jacob pressed his keypad and music pounced out of the speakers again.

Jim collected the money from the floor and placed it inside

the plastic bag that had contained the drugs. He stood up and walked slowly backwards to the lounge.

"Hey, where you going? I've not finished yet."

Jim stopped and felt his eyelid twitch. If he didn't get out of there fast, he'd find himself pushing Jacob out of the way and diving nose-first into the bag.

Jacob gave Jim a wide-eyed glare. "You and Burt are going to come along. Help things run smoothly. You get me? Ha, aha ha."

"Love to. I'll go and tell him now!" Jim beamed as Jacob went down for another line. "I'll make my own way out."

Jim came out into the blue and pink glow of the lounge. From behind him the Wu-Tang Clan blasted out again. Jacob shout out in an American accent, "Boo ya, homeboy! Jacob Little ain't nuttin' to fuck wid!"

Chapter 7

Passing the steamy windows of pubs and dodging groups of office workers in Santa hats, Jim felt defeated. The blue, double-breasted blazer that Tony had lent him was a mistake. He looked like Charlie Mason if he'd stolen Peter Cook's wardrobe.

Light from The Champagne Bar's large window shone brightly, white and warped, onto the canal. Jim cupped a hand over his eyes and placed it on the glass. Lulu sat playing the piano, her back straight and exposed in a pink, silk evening dress, long sleeves covering the intricate swirls of the red-and-green Indian-style tattoo that he knew ran down her left arm. Her black hair glowed cool silver under the muted lights.

A waiter placed a glass of water on top of the piano. She turned, gave a 'thank you' smile and looked out into the audience. Jim found himself smiling back, remembering the first time he had seen her, squealing and howling on stage with her band, The Girlies, at a packed gig in The Shipwreck. A feminist punk band in heels and fake fur, they scared the hell out of the skinny indie boys. Lulu had been the first girl to blank him since The Tyrants started to get a following. It made him want her even more.

Jim walked in past the bouncers and sat down at the bar. He ordered a JD and coke and looked to the stage. A crowd of businessmen burst into laughter and sang a rugby chant as she played a jazzy version of 'Rudolf the Red-nosed Reindeer'.

He noticed a sign at the end of the bar: *Requests by our pianist – Louise Killshore*. He plucked a piece of paper from underneath it, wrote down *Nick Drake's 'Northern Sky'* and handed the slip to the waiter. He and Lulu used to listen to the song together, wrapped in the fuzzy warmth of hung-over Sundays.

He drank and watched her as she made her way through 'Silent Night', 'Jingle Bells' and 'Have Yourselves a Merry Little Christmas'. She would stop briefly after each song to sip her drink and smile flatly into the crowd.

He ordered a couple more drinks and watched the request pile go down. He knew, from counting the slips, that his request was next.

Lulu picked up the sheet and held it a little longer than she had the others. She placed the slip on the side of the piano, shook her hands by her sides, brought them up to the keyboard and proceeded to play 'Eternal Flame'.

He filled out another request: *'NORTHERN SKY' BY NICK DRAKE!* He handed the slip to the barman and ordered a double this time. Each sip hit the back of his eyes like a juggernaut, shunting his vision out of focus.

The pile lowered. The eczema on his legs began to boil and itch.

Lulu leant over to view the request slips.

"Northern Sky!" Jim shouted across the room.

Her face grew taught. Her hands froze above the keys. People down the front twisted their heads round.

"Second time I've requested it. Second time I've been knocked back!"

Lulu placed the slip on the other side of the piano, consciously not looking over at him.

Jim felt a hand on his shoulder. He pulled away.

"Hey. Leave it, will ya. I asked for my song. She's not playing it."

"I'm sorry, sir, but I'm going to have to ask you to leave... sir," said the barman.

"When I've hear my song. My song. Fuck, man..."

Jim turned back and Lulu had gone. The two bouncers from the door were lumbering towards him. Jim's hands shot up in a "You got me!" pose.

"I just want my song, lads..."

Without a word they grabbed each side of his wide lapels and dragged him, squirming, to the door where, with a sudden lift, they threw him out onto the hard and wet canal side.

"Wankers! You fucking meat heads! This place is a joke! All show and no substance!"

The bouncers stood with their arms crossed and looked down on Jim as he pushed himself up from his knees and onto his feet.

"All show and no substance? You can talk."

He turned to see Lulu standing behind him in the orange light of a street lamp, smoking a cigarette. She was wearing an oversized green parker that cut off just above her knees. The hem of her pink silk evening dress pooled around her feet on the wet cobbles.

"You wouldn't play my – *our* song."

She threw the cigarette into the water and looked him up and down.

"And what the fuck have you come as?"

They sat opposite each other in a booth at the Cuppa Café on Broad Street. At the next table an old man sipped his tea loudly. Every now and then he laughed to himself, breaking their silence.

"You look beautiful."

"No bullshit, Jim."

She dropped her head, her fag streaming smoke that pointed up from her hand on the table.

"It's the truth, babe."

"How long have you been drinking? How long have you been back? And how long have you looked like that?"

Jim smiled. He slipped his hand across the table and placed it over hers.

Lulu immediately drew up her Marlboro and stubbed it into the back of his hand.

"Jesus. *Fucking…*"

Jim drove his teeth down on his bottom lip to stifle a scream, scooped the ice cube out of his coke and pushed it down on the wound.

"That's what it felt like for me. For about three months. Then this week I was coming to terms with the fact that you might be dead," Lulu said, leaning low over the table towards him.

Jim couldn't speak, afraid that he would scream.

"Did it mean that much to you? To not call? To not even write? To tell me you were alive? I know what you're all about, Jim Vale." She looked down and then leant back. "You're all about you. Fuck everyone else."

"I'm not. It's different now, Lu. I did call you…"

The pain grew, swamping his whole hand. His head throbbed now.

"Did you?"

"You didn't answer. It was you who chucked me out because I was dealing with Burt –"

"Jim, I know how you're wired. It was more than that; you were just too scared to tell me. I had to chuck you out. I was angry with you. You said you were going to quit drinking and quit dealing when you came back from the first tour for 'Snitches', and then you went back to do it all again. You're a coward, Jim. A bloody –"

He brought his burnt hand down with a slap, hard on the table. "Louise!"

The old man growled and looked over.

Jim lowered his voice. "Will you listen?"

Lulu flicked her head away from him and stared out of the window.

"I know I fucked up. I realise that I couldn't see what we had, but…" He stopped; he knew she wouldn't accept that. "Have you seen the music papers…"

"Yes. 'Course I bloody have. You've gone missing. You think that makes you Kurt Cobain? The latest member of the Twenty-seven Club? What, with a poxy number one and a remix? Is that what you wanted to achieve?"

Lulu plopped the fag into the dregs of her coffee cup.

"Come on…" He went to reach for her hand again, then thought better of it. "Lu. Please?"

She turned and looked up at him with hard eyes.

"Can I tell you… please, Lu?"

She pulled another cigarette out and nodded quickly as she lit it.

He told her about punching Gary, about trying to kill himself, about hospital and about Dimpy's plan for him to hide for a while. All the time Lulu smoked in short bursts, gazing out of the window.

"Don't kid yourself, Jim. You're an alcoholic. A number-one record was never going to be enough for you. You should see someone. I did. But you wouldn't, would you."

Jim played with the spoon in the sugar bowl.

"You know the last time I saw you?" she said.

"The night you threw me out?"

"No. I saw you on Saturday morning TV singing 'Snitches' to a load of screaming kids and that whiny presenter – I can't think of her name –"

"Ivy Jukes?"

"Good, was she?"

"What? Those pictures in the paper? I swear to God… all that not swearing and trying to be cute makes them worse. Her publicist saw it, and next thing you know we're seen leaving together."

"Jim. I saw the picture."

"That's why you didn't answer my call?"

Lulu looked back at the window. "So what are you doing now? How can you afford to buy drinks and get drunk in The Champagne Bar?" she said.

"I'm surviving on what little cash I have left in the bank, babe," Jim said, looking down at the burning red welt on the back of his hand.

"Don't call me babe, okay?" Lulu glanced at her watch. She covered her eyes with both hands and released a small groan. "I've got to get back. I'm on again in five minutes."

"Wait. Couldn't we just go out for a drink – I mean coffee?"

"Goodbye, Jim."

Lulu stood and made her way to the door. Jim lunged after her and grabbed her arm. She pulled away.

"Do not fucking touch me."

Jim bowed his head. "Sorry. Sorry. I know that was a long shot. It was wrong. But why are you working there, Lu?"

"'Cause I have to pay the rent. Do you think I enjoy it?"

She turned and walked to the door.

"I've got plans. I'm leaving the band... I'm going solo," Jim said. "I want you to help me."

She stopped. Her head dropped and she shook it with amused despair.

"Can I give you these?" Jim reached into Tony's jacket and pulled out ten sheets of folded A4 paper and held them out to Lulu.

She turned towards him.

"I'm going to record an album with Bix Pillar. No more Tyrants. These are some of the lyrics. Could you just read them? I don't care if, well, you think they're crap... No, that's bollocks. I do care what you think about them. I've got a few ideas about the tunes, and the keys and things... but I need your help. Lu, I want you to write the songs with me."

Lulu stood in the doorway, looking at the lyric sheets rolled up in Jim's hand. "So what makes it so different this time? Why won't it go the way it did before?"

"This time I won't let people fuck me around. I won't have an idiot manager or an idiot band. I'll have Bix Pillar, and if you agree, I'll have good songs too. I have to make it work. There's too much to lose this time..."

She took the lyrics and stuffed them into her jacket pocket.

"It was lucky you decided to act like a twat on my break. I have to go." She slipped out of the door. "That's if they haven't sacked me."

"Can I call you tomorrow?"

"I've got a showcase for a publisher. So, no."

Lulu dipped down and pulled up the hem of her dress, and Jim watched her walk through the white, oval patches of light down the pavement and disappear around the corner.

He pulled her cup over and put his hands round it. It was still warm, the fag butt that had burnt him floating ugly and alone at the bottom. He looked at the ember mark, red and smudged with black ash on the back of his hand.

Welcoming the pain, he smiled.

Chapter 8

While he waited for Burt to give him the address for the next drop, he tore out old lyrics from his notebook and laid them across the bed. He closed his eyes and let his hand fall on a sheet. He picked it up and opened his eyes and read.

Waking up from a dead lock
Jump around to the head rock
Forget things that brought you down
Throw off that thorny crown.

"If only…" he said.

He pulled the top off a pen with his teeth and forcefully struck a line through the whole verse. His phone vibrated then started to ring. He picked it up and flipped it open.

"Put the TV on. Now."

"Burt?"

"Quick!"

Jim fell forward onto the lyric sheets and punched the 'ON' button on the TV at the end of his bed. The picture and sound faded in:

"*… It is believed that the troubled singer came up here*" – the reporter looked briefly at the hills – "*with the intention of committing suicide.*"

The camera pulled out of the close up of the young woman reporting. She turned to a tall man in a tired suit who was standing next to her, and pointed the microphone at him.

"*That's right. Unfortunately it is looking like a suicide attempt at the moment.*"

"Oh, shit," Jim said faintly.

"*It seems like vandals set fire to the car some days after the event. But we've found the remnants of a plastic tube attached to the exhaust pipe, a clear an indication as any that the person wanted to kill themselves."*

The camera swung back to the reporter.

"But what the police aren't so sure of is – if this was suicide, where is the body? If the rumours are true, and it's Jim Vale from local band The Tyrants, why did he do it? Was it down to poor sales of the band's last single? His family, band and fans are now having to ask themselves the question – has Jim Vale, a.k.a. Jimmy Tyrant, become yet another rock star, along with Jim Morrison, Brian Jones and Jimi Hendrix, who lived fast and died young at the tender age of twenty-seven?"

Flutters fled like rats from his heart to his ears. He pushed the 'OFF' button.

"Hey, man! You're famous! Whoo! Big time, mate!"

Jim grabbed the neck of an empty whisky bottle and threw it against the bath.

"What the hell's that?" Burt said.

Jim fixed his eyes on the glass that lay broken into curls, glistening on the carpet.

"Jim, mate? Isn't this what you wanted?"

"No. It isn't. It's what Dimpy wanted… It's too fucking early. What if they're on the lookout for me and I get spotted? I need money for Bix, for the album…" He could still smell the damp of his mother's room, see the pot of piss by the wardrobe, feel the sadness, the guilt. "I need to earn enough to get away and tell Gary and Dimpy to go fuck themselves."

"If you go back now you can get me those new producers and A&R blokes, new bands going through Brum. That's big money…" Jim could hear an uncommon edge of desperation in Burt's voice.

Jim rolled over, stood up and began pacing the room.

"Have you listened to anything I said? I'm in this mess because of him. I can't let it happen."

"Okay, son, okay. I get it. Chill out. You better make sure you're well-disguised then. Have you thought of padding?"

Jim stood still and looked down at his stomach. He wanted to laugh. Padding? He prodded the fat which now hung over his belt.

"I think I'm alright on that front."

"Can I ask you one thing?"

"What."

"Stop being a daft bastard and come round. I've got a job for yer-"

Jim hung up. He dropped the phone on his pillow, knelt down by the side of the bed and pulled out the rucksack from underneath it. He opened it up. He had a grand already. He pushed it back under and stood up. He looked over at the lyrics and saw them differently now. They weren't just a stack of words on pages; they were the confessions of a dead man he had once known intimately and now only envied.

Burt slipped a mix tape of funk and garage tunes into the mouth of the Escort's tape player and they drove into town, past Halal butchers', newsagents', taxi ranks, men lugging crates of veg out the front of stores, down to Digbeth.

"I heard about his Millennium party, yeah, man. Massive," Burt shouted over the swirling organ line of Julie Driscoll's 'Indian Rope Man'.

"I don't get it," said Jim. "There was no one round his house when I went over. He doesn't seem the type of bloke you'd want to be friends with. For one thing, he was arrogant as hell, and for another, he thinks he's fuckin' Ice T."

"He throws the best parties, man, like the best. Everyone wants to be him. That's how I became his dealer: I got talking to him at this party. He has an enviable lifestyle, mate. Enviable. Don't you think?"

"Does he? He hasn't been very creative since he sold his company, Burt."

"Creative? So what? He's loaded."

"And he's obsessed with this group, The Krayzz. Local rappers. They sound quite good."

"What? Fuck The Krayzz, man."

Burt's voice was loaded with hatred and his face was squeezed into anger at the word Krayzz, when suddenly his head twisted round to look out the window.

"You missed the road, yer knob 'ead. It was that one back

51

there…"

Jim took the next left and circled back. He rolled the car slowly past open doors of deserted factories and empty loading bays, and stopped under a tall arch of the railway bridge. To the far left of the arch wall was a dusty, black door with a white board above, across which *Jumps Gentlemen's Club* was printed in red.

Burt opened the passenger's door and turned to Jim. "You don't need to come in." He put a hand into his pocket and pulled out a twenty. "What time is it? Twelve? Get something to eat and come back in about an hour. You can park around the corner."

It was Jim's first time in the city centre, in daylight, since his disappearance. He kept his head down, looking around occasionally to see whether anyone was clocking him.

He walked to Virgin Megastore, over to the 'T' section of the singles, and flicked through the names of bands and solo artists.

No section for The Tyrants.

He found two copies of The Tyrants' second single, "Tell Me Reasons", in the bargain bin; gaudy covers sticky from all the tags applied and removed to reduce the price. They were now ten pence. Dread uncurled in his stomach and he dropped the CDs back down with the other forgotten bands of the year.

On his way out an assistant cupped her hand on the other cashier's ear and leant in to whisper something, all the while looking at Jim.

He walked quickly towards the door, then he realised he was running – past the tills, clipping bemused customers, out down the ramp, past a gift shop and onto the street. He ran into the underpass, up the steps, into a newsagent's, and tried to catch his breath.

He picked up *Weekly Music Express* and pulled it close to his face, hoping that she hadn't followed him. He lowered a corner slowly and saw her at the door. She turned and walked back into the shop.

He breathed out and began flicking through the pages.

And there it was.

A photo: His mum outside the Co-op in Hamblington. Her hair was long, grey and limp, foot in plaster and eyes drifting to the left of the shot.

It has been four weeks now since Jim Vale singer from retro indie one hit wonders, The Tyrants, went missing. …

Jim skimmed the rest of the intro and started again when he saw a quote from Lonny:

"Looking back, Jim was always mentally unhinged, thinking about it. But we just saw him as a little flaky and unpredictable. Running off in Berlin, not turning up for gigs. Things like that. And he hasn't really spoke to us much anyway recently. He's been doing a lot of drugs and drinking far too much for a while now. Which can't help matters."

Jim looked at the top of the page; the story was by Craig Beakington. He found his place and read on.

When I went to talk to Jim's mother about his disappearance, she seemed distressed and tired, not fully connected with the world around her, saying, "I would just like him to come home. Have a chat. I haven't seen him in the last five years, since he moved out…" Mrs Vale drifted off slightly at this point: "He didn't call once."

It is clear to see Margaret Vale is not in good health. She looked drawn and weak, and clearly, worrying about her son's disappearance isn't helping her condition.

The wrangle of complicated feelings came upon him again. He needed to tell his mum that he was okay, that he would be able to get her out of Viv's house. But it was too dangerous to go back now.

Jim dropped the *Weekly Music Express* on the pile and, with a seasick feeling, walked back onto the street. He checked his phone. No calls. It was ten past one.

Approaching Burt's Escort, he noticed something smeared across the driver's side door. As he got nearer the car he could see that it was blood. He heard a wheezing moan from the other side and ran around.

"Jesus, Burt. What the fuck happened?"

Burt was propped up against the passenger door. He had a white towel wrapped around his right hand, the top half of which was bright red and wet with blood. He looked up at Jim and smiled. A gap had appeared where one of his front teeth used to sit and a globule of sticky blood dripped off his chin.

"Alright, mate… Is it okay if we stop off at a chemist's on the way back?"

"Chemist's?"

"It's okay…" he said with a pained smile.

"I'm taking you to A&E."

"No. No hospitals," Burt said. The energy required for speaking clearly hurt him. He looked down at the bloody rag. "No… I just need a bandage and some disinfectant."

"You need aspirin."

"No. I've got something a little stronger at home."

Sitting opposite Burt on the sofa, Jim removed the heavy towel. The nails of Burt's middle and index fingers on his right hand had been pulled out at the root, leaving a pulpy mass of flesh at the tips.

Burt bent down and snorted a few lines while Jim went to the kitchen and brought in a bowl of warm, soapy water. He washed off the blood, Burt's arm shivering with each touch. Then he dried the wound and wrapped the fingers in white dressing.

"What the bloody hell's happening, Burt?"

"Nothing." He shrugged and admired his new bandage.

"Oh, fuck off. I could see that something was going wrong with you before this happened. You're messing with the wrong people, Burt; it's obvious."

"I'm a drug dealer. That's kind of my job."

"There are different levels of 'wrong people' and you know

it. You owe the bloke at the Jumps club money, don't you? That's why you're desperate for me to bring in the cash."

"No… it's not like that."

Jim grabbed Burt's bony wrist and placed his other hand over it, poised to flick the damaged fingers.

"Hey, what you doing, man! Don't…"

"Just tell me. I can't have any more fuck-ups in my life. If you're involved, I'm involved too."

Burt cringed. "He owes *me*, man. He fucking owes *me*."

Jim stared him out, then let go of his wrist.

"That's why I went today. To get my money…" Burt cradled his hand and gently blew on it.

"So how did you end up like this?"

"He said he wasn't going to pay, and if I asked again, I'd lose more than my fingernails…"

"How much was it?"

"That doesn't matter…"

Jim grabbed his hand again.

"Fuck! About ten grand."

"Ten grand! And he won't pay?"

"He doesn't have to, does he? He's got people to do this to me. Maxwell. Nut case, man. He's got this gun tattooed on his palm, the barrel of it running down his forefinger. And he points it at you, man, and smiles with that stupid fucking emerald flashing from his front tooth. He's got a jewel in his tooth! Have you ever seen –"

"Burt. Calm down. What happened?"

Burt looked down at the bowl of pink water in front of him. "Well, there's this bloke, a defence lawyer in town, Henry Banhart. Wants a big bag of stuff. He asks me for way more than I have in stock. But I'm thinking, get this deal cleared and I can go big time, man… the money is fuckin' good. Too good to miss. It could change my life. So basically, I needed to get some coke and get it quick." With his good hand Burt pulled a roll-up awkwardly off the table and Jim lit it for him.

"I knew one person…" He took a drag and blew out heavily. "This guy, Beatsy. I tell him what I need, but I'm a little short of cash. He's just starting up and needs the business. He knows

I'm good for the money. He gives me the stuff and a date to pay it back."

"What?"

Burt sniffed. "This is a lot of money. I'm set up to make a lot of cash, man."

"So, what happened?"

"I get the stuff and ring up my lawyer friend, but he's not answering his phone. So I go over to his office and his name's been taken off the plaque on the front of the building. I ask the receptionist and she says he's been struck off for dodgy dealing. Left the county."

Jim nodded impatiently.

"If I sold it off in small packages, it would take far too long. I needed a decent price for the lot and fast. One night I was at Jumps and Lawrence, the bloke who owns it, says no worries, he'll take it off me, and he did… Bastard never paid up."

Jim looked carefully at Burt as he lifted his roll-up to his mouth, shaking his head. The new gap in his teeth made him look even more tragic. Jim realised now what had happened with Dennis at the karaoke.

"It was you who told Dennis who I was, wasn't it? You told him so I'd have to go back and get you business from the touring bands, so you could pay this Beatsy bloke off."

"No." He took a drag. "I told Tony about you."

"Why did you tell Tony?"

"Well, I owe him a few favours…"

"For fuck sake –"

"You needed a place to stay and you got it. He wouldn't put you up for free, Dennis needed a break in the music business, so… I said you'd give his CD to the record label, that you'd help him out. Want a line?"

"No! Burt. What will this Beatsy do if you don't get the cash?"

Burt sat still and looked at Jim. "He'll… I don't know. It'll all work out, though. Chill." He took another drag, swallowing the smoke awkwardly, like it was solid.

Jim had read the papers and heard the stories from other dealers: Burt would end up shot, stabbed, beaten to death and found floating face down in the canal at Brindley Place, like all the others who had crossed the city's gangs.

Burt sat up from sofa and looked up at Jim. "Part of the reason I went was because of you."

"Eh?"

Burt straightened his back, then leant in. "Nina's been working at Jumps for a while. Before we started seeing each other, she and Lawrence had a thing going, like. Told her he would give her this and that, that he loved her an' all that shit… Well, he got her pregnant. Said it was a fucking mistake. And the next thing… the baby's gone."

"So now you're going to be the knight in shining armour and help her get some kind of revenge, as well as trying to find this cash?"

Squinting, Burt slowly lifted his arm and rested it on top of the table. "Listen. She wants to get to out of that place as soon as she can. I mean, she was asking if I knew someone who'd *kill* him… I'm like, 'Calm down, babe. We've both been fucked over by him, but I haven't enough money or muscle to do that.' Then she turns round, all moody like, and says, 'I know where he keeps the key for his safe…'"

Burt's eyes widened and he took a sharp intake of breath, nodding. "Lawrence is a cocky twat. He knows these girls can't leave. If they do, they get taken back to some Soviet shithole or get thrown in prison, like. He doesn't give a monkey's. He fucks them on his desk, man. Keeps lube and a big old dildo in the safe…"

"So, she got the key?"

"No. She couldn't take it out at night; he'd know, wouldn't he? They usually bank takings on the following Monday morning, but with it being Christmas they can't bank it till mid-week. Weekends are chocker, and being the festive season and with office parties, she reckons they'll take about fifty grand. That safe will be fuckin' stuffed full of cash."

Burt bobbed his head. His 'painkillers' seemed to be working.

"Go on…" Jim said.

"After he fucked me up, Lawrence told me he wanted a

DJ, for the girls to dance to stuff. Said he knew I had music connections and told me he'd pull more fingernails out if I didn't. Then, I thought that this could be the perfect opportunity to get someone else in the club to help Nina get the money out safely. So, I told him I knew someone..."

"Who?"

Burt flicked the ash of his cigarette onto the table and winked at Jim.

Jim felt the air rush from his chest, a sick taste in his mouth. "No way. No way, Burt. How the fuck am I going to get the money? I'm a singer. I'm a singer, Burt, not fucking Al Pacino. And I'm not a DJ either. Anyway, won't he suspect something? Me coming in after he owes you money?"

"He sees me as small-time, man. Shit on his shoe. He'd never think I could come up with something like this... Nah, mate. It'll be a piece of piss." Burt was smiling now, looking at Jim like he'd said something stupid. "He wants someone next week, for the Christmas parties, like."

Jim dropped his head down into his hands. "Fuck, man..."

He felt nauseous. Lulu's face, angry and hurt, flashed across Jim's mind – the time she confronted him about his drug dealing, before she threw him out. If she found out about this, she would never speak to him again. Everything would be lost.

"And then they find out the next day and chop my head off," Jim said.

"Stewart may be a fucking waste of stinkin', hippy space, but he is connected. He's getting me some knocked-off passports. I'm leaving with Nina for Spain the next day. I always saw myself living over there. Living the dream, man!" He took a deep drag. "And you'll be in fuckin' Finland, wrestling polar bears or sumfin'. He won't have a clue where we are. That money is rightfully mine. And by the time Lawrence has worried about organising a search team, he'll be well in with these backers, loaded from the Christmas crowd, and me, you and a couple of grand will be a distant memory."

"When do you have to pay this Beatsy bloke?"

"I got him on hold till the end of December. Look, stop worrying, you daft sod. This will be a piece of piss. Act normal, keep your head down. I don't know, work on your songs or sumfin'."

Jim stared at the matted brown carpet covered in fag burns and stains, and thought that it must have been new at one time. The years of parties and good times, the careless spillages of ash and booze had built up and now it was ruined and full of holes.

"You start Tuesday. I'll give you more details near the date. You can have the weekend off if you want," Burt said.

"Oh, how thoughtful..."

"Not long, Jimmy boy. You get to go to Finland."

"Yeah, and you get to stay alive."

Chapter 9

"Mr Johnson!"

The words were shouted across The Railway Hotel bar in a singsong way.

The lads by the pool table watched as Dennis strode over to Jim – straight back, hands in the pockets of his white tracksuit bottoms.

"Hello, Dennis."

Dennis came in close, chewing and smiling. Washed-out blue eyes set on Jim's. He leant in to Jim's ear. His breath smelt of mint and lager, his hair of gel.

"Wowed any more audiences recently?"

"Don't push it," said Dennis, teeth showing, and jabbed a fist into Jim's shoulder.

Jim slid his shoulder back into place, his arm now feeling like a phantom limb. "It wasn't a joke…"

"All you indie cunts are as soft as shit." Dennis took a step back. "Got my million pound contract yet?"

"Erm…" The pain hindered Jim's ability to talk.

Dennis's face became stern. "Just let him hear my voice. That's all he needs. I'll sing in front of him, down on that stage. Fuckin' type of market? Every type of market. I'm hungry for it. I'll do anything. Anything. Tell him that. Or I'll seriously fuck you up, indie boy. Got it?"

Dennis started back to the group, turned and laughed. "You only need the voice, mate. The voice! It's all there!"

He re-joined the gang. A large Asian man with wide, bloodshot eyes stared at Jim as he handed Dennis his pool cue to break the pack. Jim walked across the bar and from behind him heard the crack of pool balls and a burst of cheers.

He trudged up the first, then the second flight of stairs. On the third-floor landing he stopped for a breath. Tony was standing outside a door at the far end of the corridor. He turned and, on seeing Jim, a smile flew up like a Plexiglas protection shield.

"Ah! Mr Rock and Roll, just the man! Step inside my office."

On the walls hung photos of seventies comedians with sideburns, toothsome entertainers and variety bands. Tony's bed sat next to a sturdy wooden desk.

"Have you had a listen to the CD?"

"He's –"

"I know, I know. He's got a talent…"

"He's… compared to the others at the karaoke, yes, he is good. But if you're truthful, Tony, you know that's not the standard he's going to be judged against."

Tony fell silent. Jim saw in his face a look he'd seen before, in his mother's face. A certain type of fear, not of violence, but of loneliness – of some untouchable love.

"Do you know what he's been through?" Tony's eyes softened. "His adopted mum left and he was brought up by his sister. She died last year. Overdose. Drugs. Poor kid. He needs a break, Jim. That's all. Just one break. He's a good kid and the people love him… I said I'd help."

Jim nodded.

"Okay?"

"Okay."

"Thanks, Robbie; I mean, Jim… sorry, old boy. That's awfully kind. Oh, and by the way, he doesn't know that you work with Burt. Best keep it that way, what with Burt being a drug dealer. As you might imagine, with what happened to his poor sister…"

"I'll bear that in mind."

Tony's smile shot back up. "And if there's anything I can do. You know where my room is..."

Jim nodded, stood up and turned towards the door.

"Mr Johnson, before you go…"

Jim stopped, and faced Tony.

"Did the jacket work for you the other evening?"

"I hope so, Tony," Jim said and walked out into the corridor and carried on to the attic.

Back in his room, Jim ran a bath. When the water covered the grey line he slowly lowered himself in and stared up at the brown spots of mould on the ceiling. He submerged his hands and watched flakes of dead skin rise from his sores and float away from him and sink out of sight. He realised now that when the door of his car was opened and he fell, coughing and gasping for breath, onto the muddy ground that a dead part of himself, the part that was Jimmy Tyrant, had floated away with the exhaust fumes into the dark, wet forest – gone forever.

Chapter 10

"Will you shut the fuck up!"

A bowl of cornflakes and milk slammed into the wall where Nina's head had been a millisecond earlier.

"You fucking lying bastard!"

On her knees, Nina grabbed a piece of the smashed bowl from the milk-and-cereal mess on the floor and threw it back at Burt, only to hit one of Stuart's paintings. She dropped her head down, her black hair extensions mixing with the debris on the mushy carpet, and began to sob.

"What the fuck is going on? Is everything alright?" Jim shouted. He pulled his head from round the door of Burt's lounge and stood in the frame as another plate hit the wall.

Burt came out into the hallway. His eyes were bulging – he was wired. It was nine in the morning.

"Jesus Christ. All she did was suck my dick and she wants a bag of coke! Soz, mate, it's all fine. Let's go through here. She'll have forgotten about it all in a bit..." Burt placed his skeletal hand on Jim's arm, the grip like that from the jaws of a small dog, and led him to the office. There, he shut the door and slid down into his chair.

"Have you sent off Dennis's CD?" he said.

"No. I haven't. Burt, listen. Tony told me. Dennis doesn't like you. And this afternoon one of Dennis's hard-core mates looked at me like he wanted to rip me into tiny pieces and eat me alive."

Burt's eyes widened and he laughed. He got up and sat on the desk, leg bobbing frantically. "You heard about his sister, then?"

"Yeah. Tony told me. Fucking tragic... Shit, Burt, you didn't supply her with the –"

"Nah, man. No. Way. Just amuse him, alright? You need

the room."

Jim rubbed his eyes vigorously, so he could feel it, so that they hurt. "Fuck! This is getting complicated. I just wanted to make a bit of easy cash…"

"You want to make money? I got some coke, poppers and skunk needs dropping off to Sizzle. He's a DJ. I told you about him, introduced me to Jacob Little. Fuckin' Handbag House, bollocks DJ. Doin' well. Nice guy. You're playing the wrong tunes, son!"

"Don't you think I realise that?" Jim said.

*

Jim walked from the front door over the exposed dark-wood floors into the brightly lit, open plan living area of Sizzle's apartment. A large arched window at the end framed the office blocks of the city and the squally sky above. A house remix of a Strokes song for the Ibiza crowd thumped from a PA.

"You his new delivery boy then?" Sizzle smiled from under his ice-white cap.

"I'm doing some drops for him, yeah." Jim unzipped his Puffa, took out the bag of pills and put them on the table.

"You don't mind, do you?" Sizzle spilled the contents and proceed to count them out.

"Getting many gigs?" Jim asked.

"Nonstop. I was out in Faliraki, man. Last summer? Oh my God, they like to dance at that place." He looked back down and continued to count.

"All there?"

Sizzle looked up. "Yup. All present and correct. Burt's good, man. Don't rip you off." He started to place the pills back in the bag, one by one. "The people I dealt off before?" He puckered his lips, sucked and shook his head.

"Did you ever deal with a guy called Beatsy?"

Sizzle stopped and looked up at Jim. "Why you saying that? Where you heard that name?"

"Oh, you know, you hear names…"

"No… No, I don't know him personally. Know of him,

though." He carried on counting, his head down, avoiding eye contact. Jim could see that he didn't want the conversation to continue.

"He rip you off?"

Sizzle put the bag on the table and looked at Jim. "I didn't deal with him or his old gang, you understand? It's not my thing. They deal the hard stuff. Like crack and all that shit. I keep away from it. Anyway, why you so bothered?"

"Research. I'm new. Need to know whose toes not to step on."

"You'll know if you've stepped on Beatsy's, boy, I tell ya that."

"How?"

"Ha. Funny."

"How?"

Sizzle sauntered over to his kitchen. The next song came up; a house mix of 'Snitches'. Sizzle placed the bag in the fridge and walked back.

"Beatsy was in a big gang called The Krayzz with a guy called Phaser. They're a hip-hop crew too. Beatsy spun the decks good, man; lotta people learned from watching him. And Beasty's tough, you get me? But Phaser's got a rep. Back in the day, this kid, all he did was walk past Phaser, and Phaser's like, 'Yo, what the fuck, man. You gay or summat? You staring me out, yeah?' And this kid – he's not small, he's a big kid – and he's like, 'No,' and Phaser pulls this knife and slashes his face open, right there. There's blood all over… That's just for starters, man. A lot of carnage." Sizzle looked out at the grey sky. "I heard it was him that cut the throat of that kid a few years ago, over Ladywood, man… I mean, that's what I heard, you know. A big presence. They run a big crew, big part of the city. Phaser is looking to go bigger too."

"Did he kill him? Kill that kid with the slashed face?"

"What? Does it matter?"

"Right. I get it."

"I hear Beatsy's left and set up on his own. Trying to start his own business. He's no angel either. Likes guns. Likes shooting them at people."

Jim tried to look nonplussed. He turned his head to the decks, nodding. It was the same song, *his* song, one he'd played hundreds of times, but it now sounded completely different.

"You like the track? One of mine," Sizzle said.

"It's really good…" Jim nodded on the beat and smiled at the brazen declaration of ownership.

Sizzle narrowed his eyes and cocked his head. "You know… I swear I know you."

"Me?"

"When you came in I thought, I know this geezer."

The thump of the bass drum flashing from the speakers accentuated Jim's heartbeat. "I've got one of those faces." He smiled and looked down at the money in Sizzle's hand.

"Yeah. I do know you…" He pointed at Jim.

Jim tried to grin.

Sizzle would not let go of Jim's gaze. His face melted back into the smile, then he clapped his hands and wagged a finger as Jim's voice, digitalised and distorted, blared from the speakers: *"SNITCHES, SNITCHES, SNITCHES, SNITCHES!"*

"You used to work in the metal section of Tempest Records. That's it! I knew it! I used to run in past all those rockers, man, upstairs to the dance and rap section. Get some proper tunes!"

"Oh, right, yeah. That was me. Yeah, long time ago."

Sizzle was beaming. "Back in the day!"

"Yup. Back in the day…"

Sizzle kept nodding. "Seriously, though? Keep out of Phaser's way. And Beatsy's."

"I fully intend to. Hopefully I'll be well out the way of everyone soon..."

*

In the afternoon Jim took Burt his share of Sizzle's money, then he drove back to The Railway Hotel. He brought a bottle of whisky from Tony at the bar and made his way up to his room. He turned on the TV, sat on his bed and started to drink. When his eyesight began to blur and his limb started to

68

seem too heavy to lift, he called Lulu. One hand over his free ear, the other held the phone. He hummed the tune he'd heard the night on the hill as he waited for an answer.

"Did you read them, Lu?"

There was a pause; the phone creaked.

"They're good. You know they're good, Jim... Jesus."

Jim closed his eyes, a feeling of goodness welling up inside him. "You see, Lu. We're meant for each other –"

"Okay, Jim. Stop it. Before we go any further. Just stop it, and let's get some things clear. I think the lyrics are good. It doesn't mean we're back on, though, and it doesn't mean that we could be back on either." She exhaled. "So what are you going to do with them?"

"The album. Bix Pillar, remember? I need arrangements. Strings, marimbas. I need a piano player, Lu."

"I've got my own thing, you know, Jim. I've got a whole album's worth of tunes ready, so –"

"How did the audition go the other day?"

He heard her swallow, the sound of paper ruffling in the background.

"Er, he said he really liked it and that he'd get back as soon as possible..."

"You know what that means. Lu, for fuck sake, he's fobbing you off. How many times have you heard that one?"

"I know about this one. I can feel it. It feels real this time."

"What's real is Wednesday night cabaret with a bad singer, playing cocktail jazz to people who just don't give a shit, babe."

"And what makes you the authority?"

"Look what's happened to us. It's fair to say that we've both lost our way a little. We always said we wanted to write together, didn't we? This album is guaranteed. Bix Pillar wants to work with me. I'm just getting the cash sorted, that's all... We both need this."

Another pause. A ruffle of paper.

"Let me think about it."

Jim could tell by the subtle inflection of her voice that she would do it. He hit the bedside table with his fist. Pulling the phone away from his face, he mouthed "Yes" through a smile.

"But Jim, you have to stop drinking. Okay?"

"Yeah, sure. So that's a yes then?"

"Well…"

"Lu, come on. Bix Pillar?"

"Where are you staying?"

"The Railway Hotel?"

"That cesspit?"

"Can I ask you a question?"

"Yup."

"Did you know I was here?"

"No, but –"

"Exactly. That's why I'm here."

*

Stuart was bleary-eyed and dressed only in his pants when he opened the front door.

"Hey, man." He stood there with a pleasant look on his face.

"It's Jim. Is Burt in? He hasn't been answering his phone for a few days and we need to talk business."

Stuart flicked a few dreads away from his eyes and grinned slowly. "Er... It's Jim, yeah?"

"Um, yeah…"

Jim edged past Stuart into the hallway.

"Jim, yeah, I heard about you on TV. Twenty-seven. The Twenty-seven Club. Cool…" He looked sadly past Jim, then up to the ceiling and said dreamily, "Saturn returning – coming back, you know?"

"Um, no. I don't know, Stu… A Goldie album, isn't it?"

The grassy ammonia funk of skunk weed hung heavy in the house.

"Well, yes. But you know the reason you tried to kill yourself?" Stuart said authoritatively. "It was because of Saturn."

Jim sniffed and looked around the hallway. "Look, Stu, is Burt in?"

Stuart placed his hand lightly on Jim's forearm. "It takes twenty-nine point four years for Saturn to orbit the sun, Jim. If you're lucky, you'll have three of these cycles in your life. So the years between your birth and twenty-nine signify your first cycle. This destruction and negative energy you've experienced comes from the body not wanting to leave its youth. It's very common, it's not just rock stars, it's everyone!" He laughed and then said seriously, "That means you're coming to the end of the first stage of your life, my friend. Do you understand the cosmic significance of that?"

Jim looked away from Stuart's concerned stare. "Look, man, is Burt out the back?"

Stuart's hand gently squeezed Jim's arm. It seemed that he was going to cry, but he smiled and nodded slowly. "Keep strong. Just remember, next week it's the winter solstice, twenty-first of December. The darkest day of the year. The night the Romans celebrated Saturn. From then on it'll only get lighter for you, Jim."

Jim lifted his gaze up from the floor, coughed and looked to the end of the corridor. "Thank you. I'll keep an eye out for that. He's out the back then?"

"Why, thank you, man." Stuart grinned. "Sure, go ahead."

Walking into the kitchen, Jim saw Burt in the yard through the window. He was holding a blue gas canister by a stub of thick rope looped through the handle on top.

"Come on, Zeus. Come on! Rip the fucker to shreds!" Burt shouted to the pitbull at the other end of the yard. He grabbed the canister with both hands and threw it up and away from him. Zeus followed it.

Jim stepped out the back door and shouted, "Burt!"

Burt jumped around unsteadily, jabbed a hand in his dressing gown pocket and pulled out a black gun. He fell on his knees. With one eye squinting, the bandage on his injured hand darkened with dirt, he aimed the gun at Jim.

Jim threw his arms in the air. "Fuckin' 'ell. It's only me, mate."

Zeus looked up, then charged over the cobbles, growling with bared teeth. Jim turned and ran back into the house, slamming the door shut as soon as he was inside. Zeus bounced forcibly off the other side of the door, slurping and gargling as he scratched at it. Jim looked out through the small square of glass in the door.

"It me, Burt! You crazy bastard!"

"Jim?"

"Yes. Jim, you dipshit. You get hold of that fucking monster of yours so I can come out?"

"Okay. Sorry, mate, sorry… Just checkin' Zeus! Heel…"

Burt put the gun back into his pocket. He tied Zeus up close to the fence and came into the kitchen. "How did you get in?" he said, blinking.

"Stuart."

Burt pulled out the pistol and started towards the hallway. "I've told him… I've told him not to answer the fuckin' door, man."

"What the hell have you got that thing for anyway?" Jim said, pointing to the gun held loosely in Burt's hand. "You got to cut down on the old marching powder, mate. You nearly blew my head off."

Burt shrugged and then paced forward through the kitchen.

"Where you going?"

"I told him not to answer the fucking door."

Jim followed him into the hall. Burt lifted up the gun and kicked open Stuart's door.

"What the fuck!" Jim shouted and slammed a hand down on Burt's shoulder.

Burt spun around and held the gun up at Jim's nose. Burt's face was pasty and sweaty, more confused than angry.

"I told him not to…"

Burt turned into the room.

Stuart was standing in front of a large white canvas holding a paint brush dripping purple paint onto the floorboards.

"Hey, man. What's up?"

Burt strode across the room, knocked the canvas away and

pushed the tip of the gun into Stuart's pale, hairless chest.

"I told you not to open the fuckin' door."

"Burt, man, this is ridiculous! Let's just clam it all down," Jim shouted from the doorway.

"No, it's not ridiculous. No. It's. Not!"

Stuart, sleepy-eyed and bewildered, looked down at the weapon.

"You hippie twat! Wake up!" Burt prodded the gun in a little harder.

Stuart shook his head, his mouth working but no words coming out.

"Oi. What did I fucking say?"

"It was only Jim, dude…" Stuart said, lifting a shaky hand and pointing at Jim. "Jim. Look… I'm sorry, man. I'm really sorry…"

Zeus's yelping and snarling sounded up from out the back.

"Let it go, Burt. Come on," said Jim. He wanted to go over and pull Burt away, but the fact that Burt was so obviously high made Jim unsure what he may do.

Then Burt turned to Jim. He looked like he was about to say something, but had forgotten why he'd started talking in the first place. He turned back to Stuart. The paint from his brush was tapping onto the newspaper covering the floor.

"Sorry, man. It was only Jim," Stuart said in a broken whisper, a thin tear running quickly down his face.

"It was me, Burt… Come on."

Burt drew in a deep breath. He dropped his head back, looking up at the ceiling, while bring the gun down, letting it dangle at his side. He lowered his head and walked past Jim and out of the room.

Jim looked over at Stuart.

"You okay?"

"Yeah, fine… I thought he was really going to pull the trigger on me this time."

Jim walked back to the kitchen and found Burt with his head in the cupboard under the sink. He was clattering around, searching for something.

73

"This is crazy, man. What the hell's going on? Do you want to get out of this fucked-up situation or do you just want to get high?" Jim said.

The noise stopped. Burt crawled back and sat on his legs. The arms of his gown rolled up, showing his skin webbed thinly over the bones, spotted with licks of red scars and yellow-green bruises.

"He won't listen, son. He won't fucking listen... What was I looking for again?" He stared at the floor in silence.

"Burt?" Jim said.

Burt stayed quiet for a while. He looked pained and then laughed. He put his hands on his head and pulled himself into a foetal position.

"It's Nina, man..."

"What about her?"

"We're going through a bit of a rough patch at the moment."

"You're always arguing."

"Yeah, but that's just our relationship. She keeps on at me about Lawrence..."

"I don't think the amount of drugs you're both doing is helping."

Burt sat up. He looked like he should be crying, but no tears came. "I'll be okay. I just, it's been... I'm fine with all of that."

"Right, of course you are..."

Burt dropped his hands and slammed them on the floor. "I am! I'm not a lightweight. I can control it. I keep telling her that we can't do anything till you start at Jumps, you know what I mean? She's so impatient." He put his hands back over his face.

For the first time since he'd come back... no, for the first time ever, Jim was beginning to feel sorry for Burt. He looked so weak and pathetic, sitting with his ruined arms twisted around himself.

This was it for Burt: no qualifications and a criminal record for possession of class B's. He was dealing to pay his rent and now he was in too deep. Huddled on the floor, he looked like a child too ill to crawl away.

Jim sat down and put his arm around Burt; he smelt like rotting gums.

"Remember what you said to me? Not long now, eh? You'll be out of here forever?"

"Yeah… I just want it to all go away, Jim…" Burt said weakly.

"I know, mate. I know. Keep your eye on Spain. Try to keep it together. At least till we get your money back. Okay?"

Burt nodded.

Jim stood up and held out his hand, and Burt raised his skinny wrist. Jim grabbed it and pulled him up. Burt felt to Jim as if he was made of balsa wood and cotton gauze.

"Let's get this shit together? Okay, Burt? The Jumps Club. What's the plan?" Jim said firmly, looking directly into Burt's busted eyes.

"Get there for seven. You start at nine. Finish when he tells you," he sniffed.

"And?"

"I told him your name is DJ Rocco. It should be the end of the week when these investors come down and you help Nina get the cash."

Burt turned and walked to the sink, twisted the tap, stuck his head under it, then let out a high yelp like a wounded dog. He pulled his head out, picked up a grey towel from the floor and rubbed his hair.

"Then we're out of here, man. We're fucking out of this place…" he said, his voice shaking under the flick of the faded fabric.

*

The rehearsal rooms were in a converted smelting hall in the Jewellery Quarter. On the corner of the street a group of kids in hooded tops and tracksuits were shouting, laughing, smoking and weaving from foot to foot to keep warm. Parked on the road, a black Cavalier with blacked-out windows was emitting a low buzz of bass notes. A kid of about twelve knocked on the passenger's side window; it rolled down and he stuck his head and arm in. After a second Jim saw the kid stand back, flip up his hood, put something in his back pocket and swagger, head down, to the rest of the group. Jim passed them, waiting for a cheeky comment, but it never came – only the smell of skunk blown into the cold air and the sound of a beer can being kicked about.

Lulu was sitting down behind a Yamaha keyboard, a lime-green woollen scarf wrapped around her neck, the ends dangling down to the floor. She tapped on the patchwork of stickers that covered the top of the keyboard, not looking up from it.

"I think these things are holding it together," she said.

It was The Tyrants' old rehearsal room. It still smelt of stale beer and cigarettes and the floor remained sticky and the carpet worn out. A black Pearl three-piece drum kit; high hats and crash symbols bent. A grey Marshal stack with the fabric torn, exposing the speakers in the amp and a yellow Telecaster propped against it; on top, an ash tray with a pyramid-shaped stack of jiggered cigarette butts.

Jim opened up his notebook and felt a shift in his breathing as he wondered whether he'd made the right decision. He'd never written songs with anyone other than Gary. If this rehearsal was bad, it could ruin his whole plan to get Lulu back.

Before Jim could speak, she began to play.

"This is for 'Mourning, Morning'," Lulu said, reading along the sheet music.

Delicate rolling lines from the top end of the keyboard played out for the melody. The sound began to fill and swell, and she repeated what he assumed was the verse.

"You in D?" he said.

She nodded and swayed along.

Jim plugged in the Telecaster, clicked on the amp and began to strum a D chord over it. Lulu's eyes were closed, long fingers skimming the keys. She played like he wasn't in the room.

Jim continued to strum. He couldn't sing yet. His throat felt brittle and dry. He carried on playing the guitar, varying the chords, adding notes, enriching the sound, feeling a little looser with each verse. She dropped to a seventh chord for the bridge, and into a major for the chorus, then she looked up. Jim walked up to the mic and began to sing. He looked across every now and then at his book, but after a while he hit his stride and the verses began forming, and then Lulu began to harmonise.

He recalled the joy of losing himself in the fast, brutal rush of music that The Tyrants made. But this felt different. Now they were taking this invisible thing and giving it a shape and meaning with more subtly and complexity of emotion than The Tyrants could ever achieve. The music allowed them to be cut off from the world, become as near to one person as possible.

After they stopped, they sat in silence for a while.

He glanced over at Lulu. She was rearranging her sheet music with a frown of concentration.

"That's what I've been looking for," Jim said, smiling.

"It sort of worked. Yeah. Sounded okay," Lulu said, still compiling her papers.

Jim didn't look away from her. "What? Come on, admit it, Lu. That was good."

"It needs a lot of work. It's not that easy, you know," she said stiffly, not looking up at him.

She quickly ducked down behind the keys, brought up a newspaper and threw it over to Jim. A rolled up *Weekly Music Express* landed by his feet. The front cover was devoted to the new American indie darlings The Crockets, pouting and sullen in a New York bar. In the corner of the cover there was picture of Jim, his hair plastered across his forehead, red spots around his mouth and his eyes bulging and crossed. The mini-headline read: *Jimmy Tyrant – A.W.O.L. or D.O.A.? Pg 3.*

"Where was that taken?" Lulu asked.

"I can't remember... I look dead..."

"Funny that. Open it up."

Above the article was a large picture of the journalist Craig

Beakington – skinny neck, receding chin and dense sandy hair styled like Jim's before he shaved it off.

The search for The Tyrants' singer, Jim Vale, continues. The sightings of him picking grapes in France and busking in Barcelona have all led to dead ends. Now previous fears over the singer's mental health are fuelling rumours of suicide. Guitarist and co-songwriter Gary Hughes said earlier this week:

"He could just disconnect himself sometimes from a situation or the people around him. Ignore them and go off into his own world. It's what he was like when we first met at school – he was quiet. So when he punched me at the sound check in Nottingham, I knew something had changed."

"What the fuck… You read this shit he's spouting?"
"Just carry on reading," Lulu said calmly.

The re-charting of their last single, 'Tell Me Reasons', at No. 15 this week is a testament to the increasing interest in the band and the fascination with Jim's tragic story.

Twenty-year-old super-fan Wendy Turner has set up a 'Where is Jimmy Tyrant?' website, asking fans and the general public to report any sightings of Jimmy Tyrant, in this country or abroad.

"I have been absolutely inundated with letters and e-mails about what Jimmy means to them. 'Snitches' is about the lies that society tells you, that you should follow your own path, and it seems that his lyrics have connected with a lot of people, a whole generation, really, who feel the same way. We just hope he doesn't end up like Kurt."

Although there are no definite clues as to Jimmy Tyrant's whereabouts, a new lead could help track him down. A source close to the band has revealed that before Jim left for The Tyrants' last European tour he was seeing singer-songwriter Louise Killshore, a.k.a. Lulu Kill from the now defunct riot grrrl band, The Girlies. It is hoped that she will be able to shed a little more light on Jim's mental and emotional state at the time of his disappearance. Until then, keep sending in your

sightings…
    The Tyrants' new album, A Part from the Real World…*,*
is being released on Monday.

"Has Beakington contacted you yet?"

"My mum got a call this morning, wanting to know if he could speak to me or if she had any info on you."

"Did she say anything?"

"Nothing. She told them she hadn't a clue what they were talking about."

"Good."

"Why are you so bothered about being found now? This is perfect timing. The single's going up the charts, the album's coming out –"

"I've got to do Burt a little favour."

"Burt? Why?"

"Because he's a friend and he's helped me out in the past, that's why, and… it's complicated."

Lulu's eyes filled with disapproval. "So what do I say if this journo pops up somewhere and corners me?"

"You throw him off the scent."

"How?"

"Tell him I called you saying I was going to hide out in the Highlands or something. And if the cops ask, feed them the same story."

"Oh. My. God," she said with a ridiculing smile. "I thought you hated the lies behind all this? You're just lying again, Jim. You're getting a little too caught up in playing the romantic outsider."

"What else can I do? The more I want to get out, the more I'm dragged back. I'm stuck."

"Are you dealing again?"

"No… No…" Jim rubbed his nose vigorously, then looked down at the guitar. "Like I said before, I've got some saving I'm using…"

"Still using those savings? Okay…" Lulu gave a shrug, pushed the sheet music into her shopping bag quickly and started towards the door. In silence, Jim followed her down the corridor.

Outside, the night had spilt like ink across the sky.

Lulu flipped the hood of her electric-blue duffel coat over her head and thrust her hands into her pockets.

"I could eat something. Fancy it?" Jim said.

A chilling wind blew between them.

Lulu sniffed and looked to the end of the road. "I'm walking this way…" She turned and started up the street, raising a hand. "See you tomorrow," she said without facing him.

"I'm hungry!" Jim shouted to her as she carried on walking. "Aren't you hungry? Just a bite to eat?"

She threw her hand up and waved goodbye again.

There was a screeching noise.

The iridescent headlights of a car swerved around the corner onto the road by the group of kids. The black Cavalier had gone now.

The kids scattered; some girls screaming and laughing. The car was different from the one before, a red BMW.

Six kids came pounding down the street towards Lulu.

Jim heard one kid shout, "It's Phaser, man. I told you not to come here!"

Then a little kid in a hooded top shouted back over his shoulder, "No, man. It's Cheeks. Fucking Cheeks!"

Lulu jerked to the left as they flew past her, but the tallest, in a blue cap, ran hard into her shoulder, spinning her to the side. Her bag flew in the air and she landed in a twisted heap on the floor surrounded by falling sheets of music.

The car powered past Jim and squealed round the corner.

Jim ran up the street to Lulu. Then blue flashing lights swooped around the bend and the noise of a siren ripped through his ears and disappeared onto the other road.

Lulu lay with a leg underneath her, her coat blown up over her head. She was not moving. He knelt down and gently placed his hands on her arm.

"Lu?"

Slowly he began to pull her coat away from her head.

"I'm fine… I'm okay," she said from under her hood. She eased herself from off the pavement and sat up. She looked at her hands, peppered with grit and cuts. Dribbles of blood ran down her wrist.

"Did you hit your head?"

"Stop fussing, Jim."

He looked up and down the road and then slipped his arms around her waist and steadied her as she pulled herself up.

"I'm walking you back," he said.

"I'm fine, really."

She pulled away from him and put a foot forward, only for her leg to collapse under her. Jim reached out and grabbed her before she fell.

"I think I'd better," he said.

Outside Lulu's flat Jim went to ring the doorbell for Lulu's flatmate, Daisy, to open the door for them.

"It's okay. I've got it."

"Is Daisy out?"

Lulu slipped the key into the lock.

"Yeah."

In the living room Jim eased Lulu slowly down onto the large black sofa. She let out a wheeze of pain.

"You're sure you don't want anything?" he said.

"Let me just get comfortable first..."

While she arranged cushions, Jim sat down next to her and looked around the room. In the bookcase under the window he saw the worn copy of *Tender Is the Night* he'd given her for her birthday. A big book on Chanel and a few self-help books. There was a large Elvis photo album. *How to Play Guitar*, the complete set of Moomin books. Simone de Behaviour's *The Second Sex*, a couple of Jackie Collins, a bio of Freda Carlo and a thick, ancient-looking book of Indian myths and legends.

Lulu rolled back her shirt sleeves, revealing a deep cut on her left elbow.

"That looks pretty bad..."

"Okay. You can go now, thank you."

Jim stood up and walked into the kitchen.

"Jim. Bloody leave it. I'm fine."

He rooted around in the cupboard above the sink and

found a box of plasters. On the shelf below was half a bag of Arrowroot biscuits and some powdered milk. Next cupboard across: four strands of spaghetti, some hot chocolate and a full bottle of Grant's whisky. He moved the hot chocolate to find an unopened jar of Marmite.

"I think you've been burgled by some really hungry people who hate Marmite and hot chocolate."

"Ha. Funny."

He popped open the freezer door. On the bottom shelf was a clear plastic bag. Jim couldn't make out what it contained. He pulled it forward.

"Shit! That's... what is that?"

"You found the dead mice then?"

It was just one mouse, frozen, curled up in a ball. Its tiny claws were hooked over and an open black eye was visible through the condensation on the plastic. Jim lurched back.

"Why?"

"I had a snake here for a while."

"A snake?"

"Sammy moved in... He had a snake. It didn't work out."

"Oh..." Jim closed the freezer door. He grabbed the plasters and bottle of whisky from the cupboard along with two plastic tumblers and walked back into the lounge.

"I really think it may be time to get rid of it."

Jim dropped the plasters next to Lulu. He poured the whisky, handed her a glass.

"You're still here?" she said, looking at the glass.

Jim wondered over to the CD rack, pulled out 'Scott 4' and slipped it into the stereo. Strings, big and foreboding, swooped into the room.

Lulu tutted softly, shaking her head. She sipped her drink. They both sat, not speaking, just listening, cradling their glasses in their hands.

Two songs went by. Eventually Lulu spoke.

"His grandma died."

"That's what the song's about?"

"No. Sammy's grandma died."

She drank a large mouthful and poured herself another,

flinching in pain as she lifted her arm to tip the bottle.

"It was obvious you two would never get on. From his point of view, you got a record deal and his band imploded. He had nothing…"

"Dreadful news …" Jim said.

She turned to him, threw him a look. "The thing is… his nan died on her own. No one by her side…by herself. So sad." She downed what was left in the glass. Her eyes were pink where they should have been white and her cheeks shone with tears.

"Hey, Lu, what's up?"

Jim edged up the sofa. "Living on her own. At her age. The poor woman… she had no one."

Jim took her head in his hands and wiped away the tears on her cheeks with his thumb.

"I know why you opened the door. And I know why there's no food in the house; it's because Daisy's left. It's just you who lives here now, Lu… isn't it?"

Lulu pulled her head away from him, her sobs making her speak in convulsions. "They… didn't even say sorry. She comes and goes when she wants. Sam's such a fucker…".

He leant in to kiss her. She turned away and he ended up placing his cheek on hers, strands of her wet hair on his neck.

"It doesn't have to be like that anymore, Lu. I promise."

Lulu pushed Jim away, stood up and limped over to her bedroom. "I don't think I'm ready for this," she said and shut the door behind her.

Jim went over and knocked.

No reply.

He knocked again and put his ear to the door.

"I just want to say, I'm here…" he said.

He heard her sniff and a light click off.

Chapter 11

Jim stood in a pool of yellow light under a dark railway arch outside the door of Jumps. He pushed the buzzer and waited. He had been running Lulu's words over and over through his head all day, like a piece of music he wanted to understand. She wasn't ready yet. *Yet.* For what? A relationship? To talk to him? To go to Finland?

A voice fizzed loud and ready from the speaker. "Shoot."

Jim leant in. "I'm the new DJ?"

The black metal door rattled with a buzzer and Jim pushed it open with both hands. He made his way down a narrow staircase to an open doorway. Inside mirrors on all the walls made the place look twice as big as it was, and a circular stage with a pole glowed pink under the lights. Around the room and the front of the stage were high-backed booths furnished in deep-red velvet, the fabric thinning in places, exposing the stuffing.

A hoarse voice came from above him. "Rocco."

Jim looked up. On a balcony overlooking the club he saw a small, slim man of around fifty, bald on top with short silver hair at the side of his head and a tanned face. The man gave a large white, toothy smile.

"DJ Rocco," Jim shouted up.

"I'm Lawrence Highsmith," said the man as he jogged down the stairs. He was wearing black leather trousers and a claret-red shirt, two buttons undone to show a smooth, hairless chest the colour of his potato-shaped face.

"I didn't expect you to look like Robinson Crusoe." His voice was smoke-worn and full of knowing charm. He shook Jim's hand firmly, his mouth in the same lopsided smile Jim had seem a million times from record company executives.

"It's kind of my image," Jim said.

"Image... Fine. You'll be in a booth, so you won't be able to scare the customers. Drink?"

"A JD please."

"Me too. I'll have a double. The glasses are by the fridge." Lawrence winked and pointed towards the bar.

Jim found two tumblers and locked them under the optics. He walked over and sat next to a smiling Lawrence, who had settled in a booth at the side of the stage.

"Rocco. Burt said you're well respected on the DJ circuit."

"Yes. I've never really done anything like this before…"

"I'm in the process of making improvements. There's a lot of strip bars popping up in Brum at the moment. So I thought I'd make mine different. Get a live DJ so the girls and the punters can make requests. There's a stack of records behind there, too."

"Okay." Jim nodded, wondering what kind of circumstances had led to the previous DJ leaving his records.

"Now, I'm not a fan of questions, so I'll tell you straight. This is how we make our money." Lawrence took a considered sip of his drink. "Men are easily deceived and will follow anything if they think they'll have a mind-blowing experience. They come here to escape the real world, and pay as much money as they have to do so. We sell dreams. And by the way…." He reached into his pocket, pulled out a fistful of tissues and put them in front of Jim. "Take it out on one of these and not one of the girls. Okay?"

"I understand."

"Yeah?" He cocked his head and looked at Jim accusingly, waiting for a reply. He looked down at his drink, picked it up, then shook the glass in his mouth to get the last of the bourbon out. He put the glass down and turned to Jim.

"My office is up those steps, but I'm out and about most of the time."

Jim nodded.

"You don't say much, do you, son." He reached into his back pocket and pulled out a wad of rolled-up notes, picked off two fifties and put them in front of Jim. "I like that. Let's keep it that way." He winked and walked off up the stairs.

Jim walked to the DJ booth and flipped through the LPs of old, sexy soul and dirty Euro house music. He took out twenty albums at random and stacked them next to the decks ready for the evening. Maxwell, the bouncer who'd pulled out Burt's fingernails, was the first to show up. His shoulders too broad, he waded down the steps at an angle. He ignored Jim and walked straight up to Lawrence's office.

The girls strode in at about seven o'clock, hair up and in heels, each holding an overnight bag. The last girl to arrive was taller and skinnier than the others. She said "Hi" and smiled to reveal a wide mouth with a slight gap between her front teeth.

Jim worked his way through the stack of vinyl. By ten o'clock the place was filling up. He watched the girls as they posed and writhed through the same performance in front of each of their clients. And thirty minutes later he watched them rub their noses and sniff as they came out of the toilets.

The girl with the gap in her teeth was next up on the pole. Her performance was different to the others, more like a ballet dancer, her movement far more graceful and inventive. He played Barry White's 'Never, Never Gonna Give You Up'. When the chorus hit she tipped her head at the speaker and nodded to Jim in approval of Barry's sexual growling. Jim smiled back at her and nodded to the track.

As the song was coming to an end the dressing room door flew open. Lawrence came out, Nina behind him.

"Hey, *Rocco!*" Nina grinned through clasped teeth, her eyes drifting slightly as she walked towards him.

"Hey, you okay?"

She seemed jittery. Wired.

"I know he's still looking. Don't look over." She said.

Lawrence had sat down at the bar with a petite peroxide-headed girl dressed in a Stars and Stripes bikini. He was talking to the girl but looking at Nina.

Jim moved towards Nina. "What's going on?"

She fumbled with a small purse. "He doesn't like me today." She applied red lipstick quickly, put it back in the purse and leant in towards Jim. "Okay. Wednesday twenty-second. He's got some of the people coming to the club who want to take Jumps all over the county. They'll be in VIP room for most of night. That's when I go and get the money. I give it to you and you take it out in your backpack."

She looked back and smiled at Lawrence and said through her teeth, "You think I'm stupid. But I know you keep your key under that stupid Roman head on your table. You're stupid and I'm taking you down." She turned to Jim and slammed her glass down, making the record jump.

"Okay, okay. He'll get what's coming to him. Let's just do this without any hiccups. Please? Is there any more information I need?" Jim said.

She flashed a doe-eyed glance at Maxwell, who stood solidly by the door.

"What happens if he finds out?"

"Don't worry. I'll keep him busy." She waved at Maxwell and then looked back at Jim. "You're doing the right thing. Helping me. Maybe help other girls too, you know?"

Nina winked and walked down to the booth in front of them. She lifted her hands above her head and began gyrating her hips in front of a jowly man in a tight pink shirt as he clapped out of time to the music.

Jim left at half four in the morning, drunk on the free whisky. Back in his hotel room, it was quiet. Lying on his bed, he let the ringing in his ears, the tinnitus he'd had since God know when, fill the space around him, welcoming it to shut out the sound of the world.

He dreamt he was in a labyrinth. When he looked up he saw a tiny blue cross of sky. He realised that he was in some vast metropolis and the walls around him were the black and windowless walls of buildings. He was being blown down the street by a strong wind, uncomfortable and restricting.

In the distance, people started to appear. He struggled to move, thrashing left and right. He shouted for them to run – but no sound came. He couldn't hear them speak either – but he could see Lulu mouthing angry words to his mum. Dimpy and Gary were laughing, mouths huge and dark, teeth glowing like newly minted pound coins. Dennis was holding a gold stereo victoriously over his head.

Jim flew faster, closing in on the group, kicking and punching the air, only to find that he blew straight through them all, like a ghost. They were completely unaware of his presence. He looked back at them, shrinking into the distance, as he sped down the dark and endless towering city street, grabbing out at anything to stay still, to keep in one place, just for a while.

Chapter 12

The next two days he slept till six in the evening and got to the club for seven.

He waited for Lulu to call. She didn't.

He called social services to inform them that he was Rocco Vale, one of Mrs Vale's sons, and that following a visit to his mother from London he was worried about her health. He arranged for Viv to be assessed in her role as carer. He thought that they both needed special attention.

At the club that night, Jim promised himself that he wouldn't drink, but when the booze was free he couldn't resist. He played records and watched the girls dance, hoping he could put Lulu out of his mind.

The girl with the gap in her teeth performed twice an evening and Jim was captivated by her. She had grace in her long white arms and control over her strong legs as she pulled and twisted around the pole. He wondered, with her talent, why she was there.

The office parties piled in, the girls danced, the men's smiles were broad with drink and all Jim could think of was how he was going to steal ten grand from Lawrence's safe and get it back to Burt.

Friday lunchtime.

Jim sat in the Railway Hotel bar trying to refine the lyrics for his song about Lulu, "Ghost Stories", now that she seemed further away and harder to reach than ever. Distracted by the blue-haired old woman singing between sups of Guinness and drags of a roll-up, he closed his notebook. His phone rang. The caller ID read *Soc Services*.

"Hello, Mr Vale. It's Sarah calling, from Social Services. We went to see your mother yesterday. Unfortunately we had to take action and remove her from your aunt's residence."

"No. Thank you. I'm glad. So where will she be living now?"

"Because of her health and her addiction problems, she'll be at our halfway house in Dudley for the time being."

"Halfway house? Well, how long will she be there?"

"It should be twenty-four days. This timeframe depends on her response to our rehab programme and her general health. But we were going to ask you – in these situations it usually falls to family to sort out accommodation after the initial stay."

"A halfway house means she'll be with a load of ex-cons and addicts?"

"It's not like that, Mr Vale. The best way to look at this is that all of these people are suffering from the same problems that your mother has. It's what she needs at this point in time. And with respect, Mr Vale, I don't know whether you are aware that the wait for housing in Hamblington is a good three years –"

"Three years?"

"As I said, it's usually the role of family members to sort out accommodation after the rehabilitation programme. Unless you can sort out a private programme, that is. I do know that your brother, James, is missing, and I would think that this is playing a big factor in her combating her addictions."

"It's just the drinking, isn't it?"

"Apart from the drinking and anti-depressants, we found a prescription painkiller that had not been prescribed called Co-cocadin. It's a very strong drug, usually reserved for cancer victims. We're curious as to where she got it. She hasn't been prescribed it by her GP."

It couldn't have been Viv, could it?

"I really don't have clue."

"We heard from her neighbours that your brother was involved in drugs. Maybe –"

The front door of the hotel swung open. Dennis and his mates burst in, singing a Birmingham City Football Club chant and went to stand at the other end of bar. Jim turned on his stool, away from them.

The woman from social services said something but it was hard to hear her because of the chanting.

"No. No, he'd never do that. I know him too well... Okay. Thank you. Thanks. I'll get on to that as soon as –"

The phone was swiftly whipped away from his hand and Jim was spun round on his bar stool to face Dennis, the big Asian lad with the busted lip, a tubby, unshaven kid in a blue Adidas T-shirt and a wiry mixed-race kid in a white cotton tracksuit with caramel-coloured hair. The rest remained at the other end of the bar.

"I don't know what the fuck you're playing at, mate. I've given yer a fair amount of time, like. I'm sick of saying this now," Dennis said.

"Like I said, Dennis, it'll take some time..."

Dennis nodded. The tubby kid and the lad in the white tracksuit lifted Jim out of his chair and dragged him backwards into the toilets. The bony fist of the kid in the white tracksuit sliced a punch into Jim's nose. The back of his head hit the wet, tiled floor. Black bubbles fizzed across Jim's vision.

"What do you think you're playing at, you fucking beardy twat? You're taking me for a fucking ride, aren't yer?"

Jim tried to talk, but couldn't.

They all looked down on him, their lips pursed aggressively. Dennis took out a strip of gum, rolled it up and popped it into his mouth. He started chewing, then said, "Joshi told me that some bloke who said he was a journalist came in here the other day looking for you. Then the police came in. I know every other fucker in the building – where they've been, what they have for tea and how big their first dump of the day was, right? So if it isn't you the pigs were looking for, who is it?"

Joshi, the big lad with the busted lip, moved forwards with a fist raised towards Jim's head.

Dennis threw up his hand. "No more, Joshi."

Dennis stooped down in front of Jim, pulled him up by his arms and propped Jim next to the paper towel dispenser. He grabbed Jim's face and squeezed his cheeks. "There's a lot of shit going down at the moment. Gangs are warring with each other, wanting control of the city. Kids are being shot, people going missing. In here, people are suspicious of everyone. Especially you, Jim. Most of the blokes that come here don't want any hassle – they've left that life behind 'um and they are sick, *fuckin'* sick, of being questioned by the pigs. Right?"

Jim coughed and felt his legs buckle. He quickly lifted his arm and rested his weight on the paper towel dispenser. Dennis pulled Jim's face up towards his.

"Fuck…" Jim said. His voice sounding wobbly and two octaves higher than normal.

"What's that you say?"

"Sorry… I didn't know that would happen. I swear I've nothing to do with it," Jim said, and felt the full blow of Dennis's fist in his nose. The room went black for a moment… then light again. Drops of blood pattered down around Jim's shoes, exploding out in the piss on the tiles.

The lads filed out. Dennis stood at the door and looked back.

"It's nearly the year two thousand. It could be the end of the world. People need to hear me, know what I mean?" He looked down on Jim, his mouth contorted in disgust. "I heard that you're a bit of a druggie. If I find out you have connections in that world, any… Just look out; I may let Joshi have his way."

Jim made it up to his room. He walked unevenly to the sink and filled it. He slipped his index finger into his mouth, checking for any damage. He washed away the blood that was trickling from his nose and dried himself off, then sat on the bed. His heart whirled in his chest, his head pounded with pain.

He had to get out of The Railway Hotel. Not only for himself, but for the sake of everyone else there.

Jim threw all his clothes, along with his money and his notebook, into his rucksack, made his way down the stairs and into the kitchen, and slipped out of the back door. He walked up past New Street Station, on over to Colmore Row and caught a bus to Moseley.

Across the back seat of the bus a kid, wearing a New York Yankees baseball cap and an oversized black Puffa jacket, sat in silence, smoking weed. The bus stopped and a heavy lad in a silky white tracksuit emerged from the stairwell. He had a red bandanna tied over his head and a black eye patch covering his left eye. He nodded to the kid on the back seat and said, "Yo, Si-Fi."

"Wow. What the fuck happened to you, man?" Si-Fi said, pushing his cap up to get a better look.

The kid with the eye patch sat in the seat in front of Si-Fi, face cast in a solemn mask. He gazed out of the window and said, "The Krayzz."

Jim dropped his head back to listen, looking at them in the convex mirror at the front of the bus.

Si- Fi leant over the seat to inspect the kid's eye patch. "What did they do to ya? Did they gouge yer fuckin' eye out, blood?" he said.

The kid with the eye patch said nothing, his functioning eye blinking at what he saw flash by outside the window.

"Was it Phaser? Did he pop your eye out?"

"You fucking kidding me? Phaser didn't do it. He got someone else to do it." The kid said and turned his gaze onto the empty seats in front of him. "He didn't pop my eye out. He burnt it with the tip of a hot poker. Doctor said I've lost the sight in that eye forever…"

Si-Fi shook his head. His expression flashed from disbelief to serious anger. He slumped back in his corner.

"It's true what they're saying. He wants The Krayzz running things again. Cutting down crews, man. Fury on the streets," said the kid with the eye patch.

"So what are you going to do about it? You lost your fucking eye, man, seriously?" said Si-Fi.

The kid with the eye patch pursed his lips with emotional determination. "I'm out the game. Fuck it. He's getting too strong. He's walking around with some serious bling, man. Got proper cash behind him. Got some serious guns too, big mother fuckers. It's not worth it no more. Yo. Si-Fi, man. You know, you better watch your back. He'll be coming for you too. He's going for everyone."

Si-Fi snorted and sucked his teeth. "If he comes up Broad

Street, he'll be fucked, man. That's our post code, innit. Our army is strong. He's a fucking old man now; he better watch himself."

Si-Fi smiled over at the kid with the cap, who smirked back with sleepy eyes and said, "Our army is strong…"

Jim got off the bus on Moseley High Street and walked over to Lulu's flat. He buzzed her number on the intercom and waited. He pictured her in pyjamas, the calm and warmth of her bed, his hand cupping her small, silky stomach.

Nothing.

He walked to the front of the building. The curtains to her flat were open.

"Lu? It's me," he shouted, feeling a tremble in his throat.

He buzzed once more… the warmth of her bed.

And again… 'Northern Sky'.

Then again.

"Who the hell is this?" said a sleepy voice from the speaker.

"Daisy?"

"Who's that?" She sounded high. Music was playing in the background.

"It's Jim. You've got to let me in."

"Why?"

"I need to see Lu."

"She's er..." Daisy coughed.

"I thought you'd left the flat?" said Jim.

"I'm still paying rent; I stay when I want. So fuck you," she croaked. "Look, she left earlier in the week, she's staying at her mum's. Said she didn't know when she'd be back."

Jim heard a male voice mumble, "Who the fuck's that?"

"Is that Sammy with you?" Jim said.

She didn't reply.

. He looked back up at the window and saw a face sink back into the dark room.

"Fuck you! Fuck the pair of you… Do you know how much you messed up her life?"

"How much *we* messed up her life?" the male voice said.

96

Jim looked up at Lulu's window and saw the gap in the curtain close. He trudged up to the high street and caught the bus to Digbeth and Jumps. He stared at the city from the top deck. Birmingham could have been any town glimpsed hazily from the tour bus; the faces unfamiliar, the buildings new and strange. The urge to scream, shout out, tell everyone his problems came to him. Jim pulled his bag up, pushed his face into it as hard as he could and growled into the coarse fabric, hoping it would make the pain and frustration fade.

Chapter 13

"You going to play Barry tonight?" asked a female voice – Russian, he thought; eastern European at least.

He swiped the whisky bottle he'd bought to numb the pain from Dennis's punch behind his back and faced her. In front of him was the girl with the gap-toothed smile. Her chin rested on her slender arms that lay across the frame of the booth.

"Oh my God!" she said, standing up, open-mouthed.

"I walked into a door. It's nothing…" As he smiled the plaster over his nose pulled the skin of his cheek.

"Looks painful."

"It's fine, don't worry about me… I'm Rocco by the way."

He held out his free hand. She leant in. Her eyes were wide and black, liquid, her skin a chalky white.

"Talia," she said, giggling.

"No need to laugh."

"Sorry! I'm sorry, you look funny…"

Jim checked his plaster and conceded with a sheepish nod.

"Is it okay to stand here until I get picked up?"

"Stay as long as you like. As long as he's okay with that," Jim said, looking over at Lawrence, who was talking causally to a heavy-set young man with intricate patterns cut into his hair and a square diamond earring that caught the light. The man walked off with a hefty swagger and sat with his party, a group of tough-looking young men.

Lawrence smiled evenly; his eyes swept the room and landed on Talia. She turned sharply, put her weight on her right leg and gave a pout.

"Hey, what do you think, Rocco?"

"I think you look beautiful, of course."

She gave Jim a sarcastic wink and walked down to

Lawrence. He spoke into her ear. Talia shook her head. He shrugged and walked her over to a table of businessmen, as Nina came strutting swiftly out of the changing room. She made her way across the club and sat on the lap of the man with the diamond earring. He put his arm around her waist. She pushed herself off him and dipped down along with the bass line. The man with the earring eyed her all over, then gave a pouting smile to the rest of his friends.

The song began to fade. Jim knelt down and flipped through a record box for the next song. Then he heard someone shouting. He stood and looked out.

The man with the diamond earring was rubbing his cheek, smirking. Nina was screaming at him. Her hand flew to hit him again, but one of the party grabbed her before she reached his face. Talia ran over, followed by a sandy-haired man she was dancing for, backed by his colleges from the rest of the table.

The man with the earring reached into his jacket, quickly pulled out a large silver gun and pointed it at the sandy-haired man's stunned face. He held it for a while, smiling, as all his friends pointed at the portly group of businessmen and rolled around laughing.

The sandy-haired man nodded slowly, put up his hands and went to walk backwards to his seat. The man with the gun strode forward and brought the butt of the gun hard down on his opponent's nose. The sandy-haired man dropped to his knees and grabbed his face. Two of his friends picked him up and they left the club without looking back.

Nina, unable to reach the man with the gun, screamed and ran out of the exit. Lawrence arrived with Maxwell, and Lawrence began talking to the man with the gun. Amid the gunman's party arms were thrown around and palms patted hard on chests. Lawrence nodded, eyes closed. He turned and gestured to the bar. A girl came over with bottle of champagne and placed it on the party's table and then Lawrence and the man with the gun shook hands.

Within minutes the girls were back dancing and the group sat down, seemingly enjoying their night like the event had never happened.

With an unsteady hand, Jim placed the needle down on 'Love to Love You, Baby'.

At four o'clock Jim was feeling the effects from his medicinal whisky bottle and had all but forgotten the pistol-whipping incident and the pain from Dennis's punch. He locked up the booth and sat at the bar sipping the dregs of an Old Fashioned.

Talia came out. Her hair was tied back and she wore baggy tracksuit bottoms with a long, black, leather-look jacket.

"Hey."

"Hey, Rocco. Hello, my friend." She smiled and carried on.

Jim stood up.

She lit a cigarette and kept walking.

"Do you fancy a drink?"

She reached the exit and looked over her shoulder.

"I'd love one."

Jim knocked back the rest of his drink, stood up and followed Talia out into the freezing black night.

"Where are we going?" Jim said.

"I know the perfect place."

Inside The Packhorse warm booms of dub bass slid from the speakers. Talia ordered a vodka. Jim was feeling drunk but ordered a whisky anyway. They found a table by the back door and sat down.

"So, come on, really. What happened earlier? Are you okay?"

"People see one thing and think another, you know."

"I don't know what you mean."

She put her drink down, huffed and lit a cigarette. "That guy, the fat guy with..." She pointed at her ear.

"Is he called Beatsy?"

"No. He's called Phaser." She nodded to herself and sipped her drink. "Nina is late and Phaser is asking Lawrence where she is. He always, always has Nina. Nina is on –"

"Coke – cocaine. I know. I mean, I can tell." Jim nodded

quickly. "So what happened?"

"The fat man, he slap her ass. So…" Talia shrugged.

"She slapped him in the face?"

"Yes. Phaser is crazy, okay? He is bad guy…"

"What? Trouble?"

"Well, he brings bigger group of people in every week. Very loud. Makes people move if they are sat on *his* table, you know?"

Jim nodded.

"Phaser doesn't care who gets in his way to get what he wants… but he spends a lot of money there and Lawrence likes to take it from him."

Talia sucked on her fag, nodding, then slumped back. "I come here to drink. Let's forget about it, okay? She'll be okay. She is tough. Drink these and get some more. I want to get vankered."

Jim convulsed with laughter and tried to keep the drink in his mouth. "Vankered!" He wiped his chin.

"That's how you say drunk, right?"

"Vankered, yes…"

Talia laughed into her hand and then stood up. Jim tried to focus on her, his eyelids bobbing, as she walked to the bar.

She came back with more drinks, sat down and they began to talk.

She laughed at his story about his old job at the landfill site, having to collect all the condoms and tampons that had blown away, chasing them across the fields like they were unruly kittens. He'd not given any thought to this time of his life before, and suddenly remembering those days that were fuelled by hope and ignorance gave him an ache in his stomach, so he took another gulp of his drink. Talia rocked back and forth in a silent fit of laughter, snorted out loud at him and put her hand on his leg. He put his hand over it.

"So what did you do? Before this, I mean. I haven't even asked where you're from," he said.

She sat up straight and tried to compose herself, wiping away a tear from her eye with the tip of her thumb.

"I was nurse at a spa. Latvia. Saving for college. But the

money, it was shit, so a friend told me about a guy in town
– he gets girls to England." She sipped her vodka
"So, I go to the back of big truck and climbed up a ladder
and down into metal container. I was there for maybe… six
days."

"By yourself?"

"No. A girl – she was doing the same thing – a man going
to vork as builder and a boy, fourteen, his family all dead,
killed by a gangster; he needed to escape. It was so black and
cold. Twice they threw down food at us."

"Six days in the dark?"

"The smell was so bad. We had a bucket. I wanted to
follow my dream for better life. Never thought I'd be dancing.
Lawrence said he will look after me…"

"What did you want to study?"

"Dentist. I will still do it. Be a dancer until I can be a
dentist." She looked directly at him with an eyebrow raised. "I
will!"

"I can't understand why you're smiling."

"What else can I do? And I'm very, very drunk!"

She shrugged and took another gulp, then clasped a fag
between her fingers. Before she could light it, Jim kissed her.
She let him, and for a brief moment he felt her full lips cold
with ice from her drink.

There was a swift, dry cracking sound in the room – a man
had fallen onto a table, snapping the legs. He lay smiling up
at the ceiling, cackling with laughter. From behind the bar the
fox-faced landlady threw a hand up in the air and banged it
down on the counter.

"Okay, that's enough now, Pete. Time to fuck off home."

"I think we should fuck off too," said Talia.

In the cab they kissed with loose mouths. Talia opened his flies
and pushed her hand deep inside.

They found a B&B where a tall woman with citrus-orange
hair and a grey, hopeless face let them stay for thirty pounds
and no breakfast.

Jim and Talia stumbled into the tiny, spicy-smelling room

and Jim shut the door. Talia placed a hand on his face and kissed him lightly, then pushed his chest so he backed onto the bed. She lunged forward and sat astride him, her hair, full of nicotine and perfume, in his face. He grabbed each of her skinny arms firmly and pushed her up and away from him. He stood up and she lay back in his place.

"Come on, Rocco…" she said. "Come on…"

He knew what it was like to be lonely in a country far from home. Sometimes you needed to be with someone, feel another's naked skin against yours; lose your sadness in a fleeting and sweaty, heart-racing moment. Even though she had rejected him, Jim could only think of Lulu.

He watched Talia's long leg as it rose to his chest and rested on his shoulder.

He closed his eyes. He felt himself sway and then, with no idea of which direction he was going, he let himself fall.

That night Jim dreamt of his father. He was dragging Jim across a damp beach and Jim was crying, shouting, "No! Dad, please!", pushing his heels in the cold, damp sand as they left deep grooves behind them. Jim spun round and twisted, trying to break free of the huge force above him. The sand became dry and started to slope upwards into long, soft, green grass.

His dad dropped him. He looked up to see his father walking away, and then slowly descend, like a sinking ship, into the sand. Jim tried to shout "Stop", but he was too weak.

He turned back to see what he had been dragged from. Laid out before him the sea was still and black and a bloody sun was dropping into the horizon. The beach was littered with dead, charred bodies – faceless and naked, limbs missing. The sea was silent and still.

Chapter 14

Jim had woken up shivering. Talia had gone and placed fifteen pounds in notes on the bedside table. At first he thought it was some kind of ironic joke, paying him for his services; then he realised that it was half the money for the rent of the room. As he sat up he noticed he had small red flea bites all over his chest. He washed in the sink. Paid the lady with orange hair and left.

He'd slept most of the day and now he was sitting with a headache in The Little Nibble supping a coffee. He went to call Burt to check the plans and saw that he had a voice message.

"Good news, boy." It was Dimpy. "'Tell' is heading for the Christmas number one spot! Gary wants to say something to ya."

There was a scraping noise over the party sounds in the background as the phone was passed over.

"Hello, Jim. I know this didn't start off too well, but you did the best thing in the end. Crimbo number one! All is forgiven, mate! Merry Christmas!"

The phone was passed back.

"I'll come down with a limo and champers to pick you up on Monday, sunshine," said Dimpy. "We've got a lot of things to sort out, ain't we. See you soon!"

There was no reply when he rang Burt to check on Nina and the plan for that night. Burt was more than likely doing some drops in town. He hung up, paid and made his way to Jumps.

As Jim walked past the first booth to the bar he felt someone pinch his arse.

"You'd be good looking if you gave me a smile."

He spun round to see Talia sitting in the booth picking

chips out of a polystyrene tray, a smoking cigarette jabbed between her fingers.

"Maybe if you shaved off beard?" she said.

"Fuck off, Tal…" Jim said and walked over to the bar.

"Rocco, hey!" Her voice was full of hurt. "I am only joking with you. Come here."

He stopped and turned around, his neck stiff with tension. He had to loosen up. It would be stupid and dangerous to mess up now because he was frightened.

"I had a fun time last night. Apart from when I had to put you to bed," she said.

"Me too. Really. I'm sorry. I'd drunk too much."

"Do you treat all ladies like this?"

"No. Only you."

He smiled.

She gave him a smile, reassuring him that she was not offended by what he'd done.

Jim unlocked the door to the DJ booth and flicked on the light switch.

"Nina come in yet?"

"She's gone," Talia said, blowing smoke from the corner of her mouth.

A dark feeling rushed through him.

"Gone? For good?"

"Some girls work as escorts, you know? Not right for here."

He began to scratch the rash on his hand. What the fuck was Burt playing at by not telling him?

"I just got on with her, you know, that's all."

Talia stroked her hand lightly down his cheek. "She'll be okay. She's strong." She smiled and walked down past the stage into the dressing room.

Jim made his way quickly to the DJ booth and closed the door behind him. He called Burt. There was no answer. He arranged his tracks for the evening then called Burt again. There was no answer. As the girl swept past him and the business parties filled the booths Jim span records and kept calling Burt; but every time there was no answer. With each flick to answerphone Jim's anxiety grew, knowing that Burt was probably stoned out of his mind at a party somewhere with no consideration for his own safety.

Throughout the early evening Jim missed cues on records and faded others too quickly. Now he was getting angry. Their plans had been thrown to the dogs and he didn't know what the hell to do next.

At around eleven o'clock a small man with long grey hair and a low-hanging stomach walked in and looked around. Behind him stood an Asian man in a silver suit with a white-toothed smile and a shiny quiff. Lawrence hopped down the stairs from his office and shook the men's hands. Then he gestured to one of the girls at the bar and the men vanished behind the swish of the heavy velvet curtain behind which lay the VIP room.

In his haste to greet his guests, Lawrence had left the door of his office ajar. Jim's eyes darted around the room at the naked women draped over their clients clogging the way to the stairs. Maxwell was chatting up the blond girl in the Stars and Stripes bikini at the bar – but from that angle, he had clear sight of the door. Jim would just have to wait for the right moment to charge in, take the cash and run.

Then, from the corner of his eye, he saw a blurred figure rush through the entrance, across the club, and disappear behind the VIP curtain. Maxwell had noticed the figure too and he followed it, slipping behind the curtain.

Jim quickly queued up two twelve-inch Italian dance records and set the decks so they would autoplay. He shut the booth and started across the club, dodging dancers and their clients. Blood rattled his ears as he made his way to the stairs, breathing slowly and evenly to calm himself, his eyes trained only on the office door.

Just as he passed the bar a wide hand came down heavily on his shoulder. A cliff face broke off and plummeted down to the sea of Jim's stomach.

"I'm just going for a slash..." he said, looking back and smiling. "It's on autoplay."

Maxwell leaned down and spoke in Jim's ear. "Hold it in. Get over there." He pointed to the VIP section.

Jim looked at the exit. In his current physical state he couldn't outrun Maxwell. So he walked up the steps and stopped outside the black curtain. Maxwell pulled it open and walked in. Jim followed him down a mirrored corridor to a black door, which Maxwell opened to reveal a neon-lit room.

Lawrence was lying across a low sofa, clutching his crumpled white jacket to his stomach, his eyes closing with pain. The small, fat man was sitting next to him, ponderously smoking a cigarette, while the Asian man was rubbing his forehead. They were both looking down at a mirrored table where a knife lay at an angle across a pile of files, the tip of it black and shiny in the purple light.

"It's not as bad as it looks..." Lawrence said, then stopped for a sharp intake of breath.

In the corner Jim saw Nina on the floor, slumped against the wall, black liquid smeared over her face, her hair hit by a hurricane.

"Nina went a little crazy with a knife."

Lawrence unravelled the jacket slowly and looked down at his stomach. The jacket was wet with black blood.

"Go to my office..." He stopped, gritting his teeth. "It's open. In there you'll find a first-aid box with bandages..." He winced. "Go and get it, Rocco. Keep the music playing – act like nothing's happened. Okay?"

Jim nodded.

"Maxwell. Get some towels and some vodka from behind the bar. Don't make a scene." Lawrence gave Maxwell a reassuring wink.

Maxwell nodded, saying nothing.

Nina's skirt had ridden up and her legs were twisted at apposing angles. Jim felt queasy looking at her. That phial of hate that Nina had carried for so long had cracked, poisoning her thoughts and corroding her patience; she could not wait any longer for Burt to fulfil his promise.

Jim made his way back down the mirrored corridor. The

speakers thumped out a tinny bass line. He had five minutes before the record finished. He pulled back the curtain, bounded down the steps to the bar, then jumped the stairs up to Lawrence's office two at a time. He walked in, found a light switch and shut the door behind him.

The wall on the left was mirrored and on the right was a painting of a Roman orgy in an ornate gold frame. Overfed men grappled woman in diaphanous white cloth, hands grabbing thighs and breasts. On plinths around the proceedings were statues of perfectly sculpted bodies. The gods looking down coldly at the writhing mass of distorted flesh below them.

Jim pulled the top draw of the desk open and took out the first-aid kit. The bust of a Roman god's head that Nina had said held the key to the safe was on the far right of the leather tabletop. He picked it up and turned it upside down. There was no key under it. His hands became clammy and he tried to slow down his breathing.

He tapped the bottom. It sounded hollow.

A thin layer of plastic covered the base. He pulled it back and found a folded-up piece of paper. He fumbled the paper open. Numbers. A combination. He ran the sequence over in his head, resealed the plastic and put the bust back on the desk.

His eyes shot around the room. The safe was nowhere to be seen.

The track was repeating the last chorus now; big stabs of bass boomed though his head. He looked around the walls.

It was obvious.

Carefully Jim took down the picture of the orgy. The safe was behind it, a large circle in the wall. He dialled in the code – 2-9-11-5. The door popped open to the musty and metallic smell of money. There were three shelves. On the top one was a large, black, Dirty Harry-type handgun, a clear plastic dildo, handcuffs, a bottle of lubricate, a bottle of poppers and a money-bag full of coke – probably the last of Burt's stash. The shelves below were packed deep with wads of notes bundled up into portions of fifties, twenties, tens and fives.

He thrust his hand in at the fifties; they would take up

less room. A slip of paper on each bundle said *2 x 1,000*. He took six bundles, stuffing them into the front and leg pockets of his combat trousers. Then he grabbed two bundles of the twenties and crammed them into his back pockets. He pulled forward what was left of the money – it looked like it hadn't been touched. He slammed the safe shut. Re-hung the picture. Grabbed the first-aid box and opened the door.

The track was still on the chorus. It had been skipping. No one seemed to have noticed.

He walked down the steps from the office. At the bar Talia was standing with a small Chinese man. She looked up at him with a quizzical frown. Jim put a finger to his lips and made his way down the steps and over to the DJ booth.

He got in, shut the door and leaned back against it, breathing out, sweat stinging his forehead. He found his bag and shoved the bundles into it. He zipped it up and tied the string sealing the top of the bag. With great difficulty, he changed the record. Then he grabbed the first-aid kit, shut the booth and made his way to the VIP room.

The room was thick with smoke.

"I got some bandages and some antiseptic…" Jim said, opening up the box and taking out a tiny roll of gauze.

The Asian man was looking down on Lawrence and shaking his head, as if Lawrence were a flat tyre that needed to be changed.

"I don't think that's going to touch the fucking sides, lad," said the fat man.

Nina gave a moan and her head rolled down to her shoulder.

"She okay?" Jim said to the fat man.

"Crazy fucking bitch stabbed him in the gut…" He turned and threw his tiny foot sharply into her side. Nina made a gasping noise.

"Hey, come on, man…" Jim said loudly, his hand reaching out to stop him.

The man lunged at Jim, grabbed him by the throat and growled, "You be fucking quiet!"

There was a faint moan from the sofa and they all looked

down at Lawrence. The towel was now black, blood pooled between his fingers and his eyelids were fighting gravity.

"Okay. Okay. Calm down…" the Asian man said, getting his phone out of his pocket and starting to dial. "My cousin has a car hire company here. Limos. I'll call him."

The fat man let go of Jim and sat down. He leaned to his right and, with a bloody hand, took a business card out of his back pocket.

"Wait outside and call the number on that card when the limo gets here. If you see the pigs, anything like that, call me. And get Maxwell in here. We'll need his coat."

Jim nodded and walked back down the corridor. He pushed through the curtain, glanced over at Maxwell and motioned with his thumb at the VIP room.

As he passed Talia he whispered in her ear, "Come with me…" and then carried on walking towards the booth.

Talia stood up and followed him. He pulled her into the booth and shut the door behind her.

"I haven't got time to tell you everything, but Nina's done something really fucking stupid and –"

"What? What's she done?"

"She's stabbed Lawrence." Jim grabbed Talia by her arm and pulled her closer. "Me and Nina had been planning something. But she got messed up and the whole plan's gone to shit…" He dropped to the floor, grabbed his rucksack and began to open the cord.

"Rocco, this sounds scary… "

He pulled out two grand in twenties, clutched Talia's hand and shoved the cash into it. She looked down at the money, then up at him.

"Take it. Put it in your purse along with whatever you earn. You won't get checked tonight. Take it and go."

"What about Nina, Rocco? I have to take her –"

"Nina's gone for good, Tal. Get out of town. Get to uni. Whatever. It'll be dangerous to stay working here. It's not much, but it should give you some time to figure out some stuff."

She nodded slowly.

"Keep the music playing. People will start to ask questions otherwise."

She rubbed her nose and sniffed. Her eyes brimming with tears, she looked over at the mixing desk. "I don't have a clue, Rocco."

"It's easy."

He showed her the stack of twelve-inches and how to set up the autoplay.

"So you'll be okay?"

"Yes."

"Promise me?"

"Rocco."

"Yeah?"

"Time to fuck off. Now."

He kissed her cheek. Slung the bag over his shoulder, pushed the door, then stopped. He turned and looked back.

"And my name's not Rocco. It's Jim. Jim Vale. I had to tell you that, I'm sorry if –"

"Jim just leave. Quickly!"

Jim strode through the crowd, ran up the steps and stepped outside into the freezing, black night. A stretched white limo curled around the corner of the street. Jim pulled out the phone and rang the number.

The fat bald man and the Asian man with the silver suit carried Lawrence out. He hung between them like a limp drunk. They turned and let Lawrence fall onto the back seat. The fat man ducked into the passenger's side, the Asian man in the front. The doors slammed and the limo rumbled off onto the main road.

Jim waited a second for the sound of the car's engine to disappear, then he started to run in the other direction, towards the city centre. He held on tightly to the straps of his rucksack. With a rusty taste in his mouth and his lungs burning, he reached the ramp at New Street Station.

He got his breath. He felt light headed; the image of Nina bent and broken flashed on and off in his mind, coupled with the feeling of anticipation at finally ending this sickening farce he had been involved in. He hailed a cab for Balsall Heath, to go see Burt and set them both free.

Chapter 15

The air-con pumped out stale heat and the smell from the six Odour-Trees swinging from the rear-view mirror made his eyes water. Jim held the bag tightly on his knees.

Past Edgbaston Cricket ground, over the roundabout, the driver went to turn left to Burt's street. "What's going on here, mate?" he said, looking into the rear-view mirror at Jim like he had the answer. The taxi slowed down as it approached the road.

Yellow-and-white police tape ran across the entrance. An officer, puffed up in layers of clothing and a high-viz jacket, stood in front of it.

The driver pulled up and wound down his window. The policeman leant in.

"Do you live down here, sir?"

"What's happened?" said Jim.

"There's been an incident."

"What?" the driver said, suddenly angry.

"There's been a shooting."

Jim knew what had happened: Burt's time had run out.

"Sir, do you live down here?" the officer said, looking over at Jim.

Jim spurted out, "A shortcut. I asked the driver. To take a shortcut…"

The policeman sniffed and held his stare on Jim. The engine pulsed and voices crackled over the walkie-talkie. He narrowed his eyes. Jim pulled his bag closer to his chest.

"A shortcut?"

"To Greenfield road…"

"Okay." The policeman looked down to the side of the car. "Okay. You have to go through Moseley."

"Okay. Okay. Okay!" The driver threw a hand up, nodded

vigorously, and wound up the window.

As the car turned back Jim looked over his shoulder. The whole street was warped in blue police light, like it was underwater. Families stood in their dressing gowns outside their front doors. The taxi drove away and Jim caught a glimpse of white dreadlocks as Stuart's head was lowered down into a police car parked outside Burt's house.

Jim felt like he'd been winded from a huge punch in the chest.

Burt was dead.

"The world is changing, my friend. This is drugs," the driver said loudly, tapping his head. "All about drugs. They don't want to be themselves, they want to get out of their minds. What is wrong with the one they have? What is wrong with prayer? Eh?" he said and clicked the radio. The car filled with the sound of a woman, singing mournfully over a spritely played violin.

Burt was dead.

And he now had a bag full of Burt's money, money that belonged to Beatsy. Money that Jim had stolen from a heavily bleeding man with some dark and seriously dangerous connections.

"Where you want to go, mate? Where you want to go now?" the driver shouted.

"The Railway Hotel, please."

He walked around to the rear of The Railway Hotel, through the back door, into the kitchen, and ran up the stairs.

His room was cold and the smell of damp was more prevalent than ever. He slowly closed the door behind him and threw on the light. He walked in as quietly as he could and picked up the empty bottle of JD on the bedside table. He held it above his head, kicked open the bathroom door, and screamed "Argh!", then waited.

No one.

He walked in slowly and looked around.

He checked under the bed and behind the curtain.

No one.

He paced up and down the length of the room. Thoughts of who killed Burt and what the fuck he was going to do next bounced around his head like angry wasps caught in a jam jar.

He went over to the window and leant his forehead on the cold, dusty glass and looked out. No cars, no activity from the train station.

Then his bag began to buzz.

Jim stared at it for a moment. He breathed in, ripped open the flap and pulled out the phone.

"This Jim?" the deep voice said urgently.

"Yeah. It's Jim. Beatsy?"

"I want my money."

"Why you calling me?"

"You know. You know what's happened. You're the next one to go too."

Jim looked out of the window. Up and down the street. Empty.

"Why the fuck did you –"

"Hey! This can be easy. Do as I say and it will be all okay."

Jim took in a measured breath, held it, then blew out slowly. "Sure. Let's get this sorted."

"Good. Good. Right answer. You know the big car park by The Royal George pub?"

"The one they're going to knock down?"

"You got the fuckin' money?"

"Yes."

"Third floor, in the next hour. You and the money – no one else, you get me? If you don't turn up, I'll come and find you. You won't see the *fuckin'* next century. "

The line went dead.

Jim put the phone down on the bed and counted out what he'd taken. After Talia's cut, and laying aside half for Nina, he had fourteen grand. Ten grand was for Beatsy, which left Jim four thousand to add to the nine and a half thousand he already had for his record fund. He took off a pillowcase and stuffed his money into it. He went into the bathroom, knelt by the side of the bath and pulled open the side panel. He stuffed the pillowcase containing the money tightly under the bath and slid the panel back in place. He picked up a plastic bag from by the sink and packed in Beatsy's money. He lowered the package into his rucksack and tied up the cord. Then he threw the bag onto his shoulder, walked out of the room, shut the door behind him and tried to block out the thought that he may not get the chance to come back and pick his money up.

The multi-storey car park loomed black against the grey and purple sky. Tarpaulins hung over its decaying concrete like loose bandages. The mesh fence that surrounded the building had been pulled away at the entrance ramp. Jim walked up and in, trying to fix his eyes, to focus in the dark.

The wind played the tarpaulins like slackened drum skins, the wheeze and flap amplified by the car park's hollow body.

"Hey!" he shouted.

Nothing. Just the strain of his thin echo.

He turned up to the second floor.

He couldn't hear a car engine or even any voices.

A sheet on his left billowed out like a sail and light fell across a pile of torn cardboard. At one end a pair of ravaged Reeboks poked out, surrounded by used needles and beer cans. He pulled down tightly on the bag and ran up the last ramp to the third floor.

No car. Just yellow and black shadows making the floor resemble tiger fur.

Jim's phone rang out loudly. He fumbled quickly, pulling it out of his pocket.

"Hello –"

"See that red chute?" The same voice as before; slow and precise this time.

A tube used to slide rubble to the ground floor was hanging over the side of the building.

"Yeah. Where the fuck are you, man? I thought..." Jim said, turning three hundred and sixty degrees.

"Shut up. Throw the money into that tube. Hear it drop. Wait for us to drive away, then go."

"You said –"

"Shut. The fuck. Up. I'll call you tomorrow. We need to talk. If we don't – let's just say we know were Lulu lives. Get me?"

The line went dead.

The whole building was creaking like a ghost ship in a storm.

Jim ran over to the corner and threw the bag in the mouth of the shoot. He listened to it rattle down the tube.

A quick turn behind him – still clear.

He leant over the balcony and saw the murky outline of a car at the rear of the building. He heard the bag hit the floor and he pushed himself back.

A scrabbling sound.

A car door slammed; a wheel spin scored the air.

Jim crouched by the balcony and peered over to watch the car tear off around the bend and onto the road. Was it the black Cavalier that had been outside the rehearsal room the other day? It was impossible to tell in such limited light.

He pulled out his phone and called Lulu's flat. No one answered. After the third attempt someone picked up.

A sleepy female voice said, "Who the fuck is this…"

"Lu?"

"Jim? Again? I've told you she's not here. Now fucking leave me alone."

He felt himself losing it, the reality of what was happening sending the muscles in his stomach and groin into spasms.

"Daisy. This is important. You've definitely not heard from her? Has anyone apart from me been asking for her? Anyone come to the flat?"

Daisy growled. He could hear her moving, maybe sitting up. "No… but –"

"But what?"

"There was this car parked outside a few days ago, not long after you left."

"Can you remember what colour it was?" There was panic in his voice now.

"What?"

"What colour was the car, Daisy?"

"Jesus, chill the fuck out, Jim. It was a dark colour, black, I think. Could have been blue. I can't really remember."

"Okay. Daisy, look. I know you hate my guts and the feeling is mutual, but if she does come back, or if anyone comes calling for her, make sure she calls me. No, better still, tell her to go back to her mum's. Okay?"

"Why? Why all this cloak and dagger shit?"

"Just do it. Or she could be in danger."

"Who are you? Luke Skywalker?"

"Just fucking do it, Daisy."

Jim pressed 'End Call'.

Jim bolted back down the floors, past the heap of cardboard, through the opening in the fence and out onto the road. He kept running to the Rag Market, weaving in and out of empty stalls; a soup van surround by a crowd of homeless people – the smell of stew – he hadn't eaten since lunch and he suddenly realised how hungry he was. Jim stopped and looked back at the van. A scuffle broke out over portion size. It was five forty in the morning. He decided to carry on, try and keep warm till McDonalds opened; maybe try and find a greasy spoon. Somewhere warm that would help stop him shaking. Somewhere that he could eat and untwist the knot that had formed in his stomach.

Over the top of the buildings the sky was washing into a luminous blue. The voices from the food van began to fade.

He heard the drilling sound of a car engine and looked back as a set of headlights swept around the corner.

He began to run. Past billboards and factories. Under the Aston Expressway.

The revs behind him got louder.

The car park he ran onto was dark and empty. Nowhere to hide. He kept running.

The car swerved in front of him, skidded and stopped dead. This was not the car that had taken off with the cash. This was a white Jeep.

The driver's side door flew open. Maxwell got out with a

crowbar in his hand and strode towards him.

"Do not move," he said.

Jim looked around and put his hands up.

"Hey, Maxwell." He smiled. "I thought you were the TV licence man."

Maxwell flashed his emerald tooth, pulled the crowbar back and slammed it down into Jim's thigh.

Jim hit the ground instantly, his leg hot and lifeless.

Maxwell grabbed Jim's collar, dragged him to the Jeep and threw him like a rag onto the back seat, then he got in himself and drove off.

It wasn't long before Maxwell pulled up on a plot of waste ground next to a disused train station. The limo that they had taken Lawrence in was parked next to a wall covered in graffiti.

Maxwell dragged Jim, limping, over to the limo. A side door opened and he was pushed in.

"Where the fuck do you think you're going, sunshine?"

Jim looked up from the floor to see the fat man and the Asian man in the silver suit sitting on the back seat. The fat man had blood smeared on his shirt, across his belly. The Asian man smiled wearily and tutted.

Jim held on to his leg and tried not to look at them. The hard sole of a shoe kicked his shoulder so that he rolled onto his back.

"I just wanted to get out, fellas. I play music, okay? I don't want to be mixed up in this –"

"Shut up, dickless," the fat man said, and drew his hand down over his face in frustration.

"We don't want anything to do with this gangster shit either, Rocco," said the Asian man. "We've done nothing wrong. We don't work the way Lawrence does. It's not our style. We're a legitimate investment company. Businessmen. Okay? If we play this properly, no one, apart from that girl who stabbed Lawrence, will be implicated."

Jim pushed himself up and sat on the seat opposite. The car smelt of disinfectant and cleaning products.

"Where is she?" he said.

"Maxwell's going to go back and drop her at the hospital."

"How's Lawrence?"

The Asian man looked over at the fat man and the fat man looked at Jim.

"Look, as I said, Bernard and I, we're a legitimate company; we don't –"

"Yes, you fucking told him that two fucking times now, Paul," the fat man said.

"There's no need to worry about Lawrence…" Paul said.

Bernard lit a cigarette, pulled on it and blew the smoke out over Jim. "Now. If you were thinking of going to the police –"

"I wouldn't. I don't care about Lawrence. He was a total cunt to those girls – she did the right thing. I just don't want to be part of all of this. That's all."

Bernard nodded in agreement and smiled. "After he's dropped off the girl Maxwell is going back, and with the help of Paul's family he'll be blitzing that room of any evidence we were there. Got it?"

"This could be very bad for our business, Rocco," Paul said.

"So, the plan. We don't want any more bodies – but if you mention that we were there tonight… well, there may just have to be," said Bernard, stubbing out his fag in the door's ashtray.

"Deal. That sound like a deal," Jim said.

"If the police do get you, you tell them we were waiting for Lawrence to start our meeting. Okay? And don't ever come back to the Jumps club or visit any of the girls ever again. You got that?"

Jim nodded.

"If you do," Bernard continued, leaning forward towards Jim, "you won't be seeing another Christmas morning ever again. So remember: if we're not mentioned, that means you're not either."

The door opened and Maxwell dragged Jim out onto the broken-up soil and clumps of sharp concrete. As he lay shivering on his side he heard the fat man say, "Okay. Do it, Max."

The car door slammed and the limo drove off.

Looking up, Jim saw Maxwell's huge body mass blocking out the sky, dreadlocks dangling towards him. Maxwell reached down, pulled Jim up like a weed from the dirt and slammed him against the wall. He spun Jim round and pinned his arm against his back; it felt like his arm would snap at any moment. He grabbed Jim's hand.

"Please... not my fingers. Please don't break my fingers."

Maxwell clasped hold of Jim's little finger and began to bend it back.

"No... Please. I won't –"

The pain was too much for him to speak. The finger was nearing the cuff of his Puffa jacket.

Just when he thought Maxwell was going all the way, he felt his finger spring back and his arm dropped. He turned and looked up at Maxwell's stony face.

"If we see you again or you talk, you'll lose all your fingers. You'll just have two balls of skin for hands."

Jim nodded and tentatively rubbed his limp shoulder. "Sure... I would never..."

Maxwell shook his head in disgust and spat on Jim's shoes. He walked slowly back to his Jeep. He got in and drove, wheel spinning, through the glowing, shallow puddles and out of the deserted plot.

Chapter 16

In MacDonald's by New Street Station, Jim ordered a Big Breakfast with an extra hash brown and a large coffee. The whisky had worn off about an hour ago and the pain in his leg was starting to rise to a higher register that cancelled out the ache in his finger and arm.

Over sips of bitter brown coffee he watched tramps amble in with dull tinsel wrapped around their necks, buying burgers with loose change from yesterday's Christmas shoppers.

Folded up on the table was the *Birmingham Gazette*. Jim opened it out. The headline read: *Gang Wars on Broad Street. Man, 19, stabbed in local gang fight over drugs outside a chip shop*. A photo showed the victim as a young boy, dressed in his green school uniform, looking into the camera with a shy smile. The paper said he was called Simon Finlay, known as Si-Fi, a member of the gang The KFC crew, so called because they would meet up in the car park of the fast food restaurant. Friends and family were quoted as saying that he was a much loved member of the community.

Jim recognised the victim as the kid with the headphones smoking weed at the back of the bus the other day. He knew why Phaser had done this in front so many people, on one of the busiest streets in Birmingham. It was a publicity stunt – another example to the other gangs in the city as to what happens when you cross The Krayzz path.

The Krayzz army, it seemed, was getting stronger by the day.

By trying to sell drugs in the city centre Burt had been caught up in Birmingham's biggest gang war in years. And now Jim was too.

Jim pushed the paper away from himself when the crackle and beep of tinny radio voices came into the restaurant.

Two police officers.

The first, tall and bony faced, took off his helmet. His head popped up out of his thick jacket like a tortoise's from its shell. Next to him, the short, plump policewoman's face was flushed pink from the cold. After they picked up their orders they took a seat opposite Jim on the other side of the room.

Jim's phone said 07.05. It was too early to call Bix or Lulu.

He took another bite and looked up.

The woman had her hands around the paper cup in front of her and was looking directly at Jim. She dropped back a little and said something out of the side of her mouth to her partner. He was just about to take a bite of his burger but stopped to gaze over at Jim.

Jim pushed the rest of the coffee away and stood up slowly. He stretched and yawned. He picked up the phone and walked, without urgency, towards the door, straight past them, feeling their stares boring into his back as he exited the building

Outside he quickened his steps down a ramp towards New Street. Halfway down he turned and saw the two officers behind him zipping up their jackets. He sped up. Reaching the bottom of the ramp, he turned left. Looking back, he saw they'd picked up their pace to a jog. The woman was talking into a walkie-talkie on her collar.

Jim whipped his head round and started to run, battling the searing shot of pain from Maxwell's crowbar hit. Under the walkway, past the Christian book shop, past the Afro-Caribbean hairdresser's, past the chip shop. He looked back – the policeman was in front of his partner now. Heart rattling, Jim took a left up the ramp into the train station car park.

Footfalls echoing, thuds and squeaks, heartbeat banging in his ear.

From behind he heard the policeman taking in sharp breaths, the clanking of handcuffs and a baton.

His leg cramping up now. Hard to breathe.

Up onto the first floor. He could carry on up, or take a right and go back down. Or he could take the stairs.

As he limped towards the stairwell, the door flew open. The policewoman walked out. He zagged to his left for the ramp, then felt his legs being swept from underneath him. His arms flew up. He hit the ground on his side, his head cracking down onto the tarmac.

"You didn't look like a runner." The words fell hot on his neck.

His arms were pulled behind his back. A knee speared him in place on the cold, hard floor.

"Please…" Jim tried to breathe. "Please. I haven't done anything wrong."

"Are you sure about that?" The woman said in a Geordie accent.

Jim heard the click of a walkie-talkie.

"Yeah. We've found him," the man said. "The pop star. Jimmy Tyrant. Er, James Vale. Where? Eating breakfast in MacDonald's. Looks like that's all he's been eating for the last month, by the size of him."

The woman pulled open Jim's backpack and took out something that Jim couldn't see – the angle was too steep.

"Er, Sarge, we're bringing him in," the man said.

A fuzzy, undecipherable reply came from the radio.

"Yeah… Sergeant Doyle clocked him. I hadn't got a clue who he was."

His hands in cuffs behind his back, Jim was escorted by the officers through the station and into an interview room at the end of a white tiled hallway. They jammed him into a chair in front of a desk and slammed the door shut behind them. On the other side of the desk was a bulky man, reclining back in his seat, his hands behind his head. He was wearing a charcoal-grey suit. His cheeks were pock marked and he eyed Jim as he scratched the top of his head with the tips of his fingers into the fizzy, blond hair that thinly smattered his scalp.

"Okay. Mr Vale. Good job, Sergeant Doyle. If it wasn't for this mad music fan, we'd never have found you."

"They're a good band, The Tyrants." Sergeant Doyle sat in the corner behind Jim.

"I'm Detective Inspector Craven, and I'll be conducting this interview. That's Sergeant Doyle and the man in the other corner is Detective Sergeant Adrian Green. And you are James Vale, right?"

The DI pushed forward a folder and opened it to a picture of Jim in his Puffa jacket and his full beard, along with a newspaper cutting from the *Birmingham Post*. The headline read: *Yeti! Found! Or is it Jimmy Tyrant?*

Jim had a bandage across his nose; the photo must have been take in the last few days.

"After Mr Dimpleton told us you'd gone missing in Nottingham, and because of the circumstances in which Mr Dimpleton's car was found, we were this close to putting you down as suicide. According to Sergeant Doyle, it seems to be the choice way to go in the music industry. But we couldn't locate a body."

He looked over Jim's shoulder and nodded at Sergeant Doyle. He pushed the file away and leaned in. "We did a sweep of local hospitals and found you listed as being in A&E at the Queen Elizabeth. Apparently you were dumped outside. The car was leaving the gates when they found you. You were discharged two days later and no one has seen you since. We filed it. It was going to be an on-going case. Missing persons. All of that changed when the keen eye of young Sergeant Doyle over there spotted you. That is how we know who you are, Mr Vale."

The DI shot up out of his chair. Tall and heavy, his wide hands on his hips, he looked down on Jim. "We found you. The band will be pleased. Now, more importantly, how well did you know Marion Parker Baines?"

"Who?"

"You may have known him as Burt?"

"Marion?"

The detective put a finger to his lip and began pacing the small room. "Yes. Marion. He was shot dead last night. Your reaction is pretty much the same we've had from everyone we've interviewed. We know you knew him, Jim."

"Yeah, I lived with him… friends for a while."

"Where were you between nine o'clock last night and twelve o'clock this morning?"

"I was, er, I was DJing at a club –"

"Which club?"

Jim sniffed and looked down. "Jumps."

"Can you confirm this? We can call the owner?" Green said, now standing beside Craven.

Jim lifted his head. "Yeah… Call them… They know me as DJ Rocco."

Craven nodded with a faint grin and wrote something down on an official-looking pad.

"Little down on your luck recently, so Sergeant Doyle tells me. Your last song didn't do very well. Talk of you experiencing mental health problems?" said Craven.

Jim turned to Sergeant Doyle. He could see that she had a small hole in her nose where a ring used to be.

"It was in the *Weekly Music Express*. Gary said you'd get frustrated over little things and fly off the handle with him. Mood swings. Didn't know whether it was drugs or just you."

Craven stopped pacing. "Since you've been away, your friend Burt's business has become considerably more active. He was supplying all the big venues and the bands that passed through. Did the toffs as well. The lawyers, accountants…"
He bent down sideways into Jim's view. "Eh? You knew that, though. Didn't you?"

"I've been away for a long time."

"And you come back and now you're washed up and you're broke. Am I right?" Craven held his gaze. "Yes? And Burt, whom, I'm in no doubt, you helped set up all these big bands with coke and pills, is raking it in. Making a shedload. Right?"

Jim shook his head. "No… No. You're so wrong –"

"We find you, the day after he's been killed, with a bag of cocaine in your backpack and you're running away from us? It's pretty good grounds for being a suspect, Mr Vale."

"Cocaine?" Jim said.

"In your bag? A coin-bag full of cocaine."

Burt always said to take more just in case people got greedy;

they usually did – Jim must have had a little left over from his last drop, stashed in the front pocket. Jim exhaled what was left of his hope. "You… you couldn't be further from the truth. It's not in me to do that; why would I do that to him? I only wanted to help him. You don't understand – I was trying to prevent all of this."

The DI smirked back at the officers. "Come on, Mr Vale. You have a very convincing motive."

"He got me a place to stay for a while. Do I look like a fuckin' murderer? Look at me."

"What have looks got to do with it, Mr Vale?"

"This whole thing has gone wrong… I just wanted to sort out some problems I have at the moment. Make things right again. I didn't think it would all end up in this mess." Jim coughed to stop his voice from shaking. "I was DJing. Burt got me the job. Please believe me, Inspector. I know he wasn't squeaky clean, but he was in a lot of trouble… He didn't have many friends apart from me. I was helping him –"

"And Stuart, er…" Craven interrupted and clicked his fingers at Sergeant Green.

"Stuart Homer, sir."

"Mr Homer was asleep, apparently, when the shooting happened. Got to say, he knows his legal jargon. He's the person who mentioned your name."

"Stuart? That fucking…"

Craven sat down, his face frozen in a cool stare.

As Jim thought about what he should say, the moment seemed to last for hours. He could lie and tell Craven that Burt couldn't pay his rent, or that his car needed a new engine, and that he was paying. But this was another lie; it was deception, and deception was what had got him here in the first place.

"Burt owed money to this bloke called Beatsy. That's what I was helping out with. You heard of him?" Jim said.

"How much?"

"Ten grand. I sorted that out last night. I had to hand it over to him. I've had a number one hit single, Inspector." Jim rubbed his nose with the back of his hand. "Burt helped me get my record deal, so I helped him out as much as I could…"

Craven looked at Sergeant Doyle and then back at Jim. Craven wrote more unintelligible words on his pad and said, "Could we do a photo fit?"

"I didn't see anyone. I had to drop the money down a refuse chute. Someone picked it up and drove off."

"Right... Anyone else you think may be a contender?"

"A bloke called Dennis. He drinks in The Railway Hotel. I wasn't allowed to mention Burt to him. A bloke, er, at the bar reckons Burt supplied his sister with the drugs that killed her."

"Got a last name? For Dennis or this fella at the bar?"

"No, sorry."

Craven looked again at his pad and scribbled.

"You've heard of these people before?" said Jim.

From behind him Green spoke: "Beatsy Lewis has been in and out of various institutions since he was a kid. For a long time he was associated with a gang call The Krayzz. Many people think that they're just are a rap group, but their day job is dealing drugs, stealing TVs and car theft. We know that Beatsy is near the top when it comes to the hierarchy of the gang, but we've never been able to pin him down to anything specific. The top dogs get the younger kids to do the dirty work. Apparently he's been trying to break away from the group recently. Set up on his own. A kid called Phaser runs the show now."

Craven picked up from Green. "And this Dennis fella you mentioned, Mr Vale, sounds like Dennis Whittle, also deals in stolen and knocked-off goods – electrical stuff; music equipment mostly."

"I got this" – Jim pointed to his swollen nose – "because I wouldn't help him get a showcase with a record label. He hates drug dealers. Has this tic of chewing, like he's always ready to fight someone. He seems pretty desperate to me. He's the person you want to be questioning."

Craven blinked slowly and nodded at Jim. "Good voice?"

"Jesus Christ... No. You think I'm trying to set him up? Have you heard him?" Jim came forward fast in his chair, angry at their ignorance. "Look at my nose! My head has only just stopped hurting. He threatened me the first day I saw him. Seriously. He said my life wouldn't be worth living if he knew I was caught up in drugs. Those were his actual words."

Craven's stare was hard and gave nothing away.

"Didn't you get any witnesses from the road? His next-door neighbours didn't see anyone leave the house? I mean, there were gunshots," Jim said.

Craven leaned back in his chair, his belly buffing the table edge, and laughed down his nose. "Mr Vale, it's easy to say the telly was turned up or they were asleep. Forget that... Look. We'll check, Dennis's file. Bring him in and question him. We'll have to get confirmation you were where you said you were at those times, and a swab for the lab. In the meantime you will be held in a cell, at least until we have a little more information."

In his cell Jim was asked to strip for a search and swab. After an uncomfortable anal cavity exploration conducted by Sergeant Green, Jim was given a blue paper suit to wear. Green handed him a vintage car magazine and told him someone would bring him a cup of tea a little later. He shivered on the metal bench under the small square window. The rash on his legs had flared up and he wanted to scratch it; but if he did, he'd tear the suit and become even colder. He kept imagining the moment Burt was shot. Did he raise his arms? Did he run from his killer? Was he even conscious? Whatever the method, it was a lightning-quick tragedy, over in the tensing of a finger – and he had been too late to save him.

After what seemed like hours walking the cell to keep warm, he lay down with the magazine over his eyes. He was drifting off when the door clunked open and Sergeant Doyle threw his clothes onto the floor beside the bench.

"Put these on. I'll be back in a moment."

The digital clock in the interrogation room said thirteen forty-six when Craven waded in with Green and Sergeant Doyle in tow.

"We checked your records. Clean as a whistle. That's good. We went to Jumps. Yes, you were there...We spoke to a Mr Maxwell Jones?"

Jim nodded. Waited.

Craven sniffed, not appearing convinced. "It looks to us that in many of these incidents it's a case of making the wrong choice in the people you hang around with. Or we could call it misfortune. Given your history of disappearing and making people worried sick about you, we could also call it, well, stupidity. The one offence we can pull you up on is possession of a class A. If we did, you could be looking at anything up to seven years."

Green looked sternly at Jim and nodded along with Craven.

"There is a way, though, Jim. Sort of trade that problem," Craven said.

Jim breathed in deeply. He knew he had no other option now. "What would I have to do?"

"We've talked to Dennis Whittle and ruled him out. He was engaged in other activities that night. We have at least ten witness saying that they saw him in the bar of the Railway Hotel. We're positive about that."

"You are?"

"Yes. It seems he was spending the evening with a Tony Oscott who runs The Railway Hotel."

Jim nodded.

"Beatsy's a key figure in the rise in the gangs in the city and he's someone we've wanted to pin down to dealing for a long time. At the moment we've got nothing substantial, but if we get him to admit to killing Burt, well, then we may be able to overlook these little problems of yours. And you get to take down a real bad guy and get to the heart of why all these young men in gangs are killing each other. How about that, eh, Jim?"

Craven looked over at Jim, clicking his tongue in his cheek. "So let's reiterate. You've had no physical contact with Beatsy? Never met him?"

"No... but he did say that he wanted to call me... said if I didn't answer, he knew where my girlfriend, well, my ex-girlfriend, lives."

Craven sat down in front of Jim and sipped his tea. The

paper cup looking like a thimble in his hand. "Good. That's good. So this is what we'll do: you arrange to meet him somewhere. We have a couple of unmarked cars round the building –"

"I need a fag."

Craven pulled out a packet of Embassy. He slid one out and rolled it towards Jim, then gave him a lighter.

Jim lit the cigarette and blew out.

"Jim, you realise you could be looking at a serious stretch. Dealing is serious stuff. Real-life serious stuff. Your friend, Burt, is dead because of it."

Jim took another drag. He knew they were right; he'd just never thought it would have come to this.

Craven leaned back and exhaled patiently, looking between Jim and Green.

Jim drew his last drag and stubbed out the rest of the cigarette. "Okay. If this means my girlfriend – my ex-girlfriend and my family won't get hurt, and you can get hold of the man who killed my friend, I will."

Craven stood up, nodding and scratching the back of his head. "Good man, Jim. Good man." Craven sat down and spoke directly to Jim. "Okay, this is what'll happen. You'll meet up with Beatsy. The likelihood of you being able to choose the venue is slim. Take something with you, dope, coke… Show some nouse, it'll be respected. Set a time. Ask him what he wants. If you were Burt's only friend, he's thinking that you'll be taking over the business and more than likely wants to discuss future business deals. Or, now that you've a bit of money from the record, he may want some of that… Hand over the drugs as a symbol of good will, and then when he has them, we can take him in."

Jim leant over for another cigarette. "God's sake…" he muttered.

"What's that?" Green said.

Jim placed his head on the table. "I only wanted to sell some records… Make things right."

"You've said. Look, at least two more people know about The Tyrants. Sergeant Green and I had never heard of you before today." The DI looked over at Green and winked.

"He's getting quite big again though now, Sarge. A cult figure type, like Syd Barrett – you know, from Pink Floyd," Sergeant Doyle said. She turned to Jim. "Loads of stories about you out there saying you've become a member of the Twenty-seven Club."

"What club's this, Sergeant Doyle?"

"Twenty-seven years old. All the greats – Jimi Hendrix, Jim Morrison, Kurt Cobain – they all died at twenty-seven. Lived life to the full and then checked out."

"Bloody idiots," Green said quietly to Craven.

Jim looked up, his eyes shot red. "It's not like that." He drew in a sharp intake of breath. "When I hit twenty-seven it was like Jimmy Tyrant, this person I'd created, was taking over... I couldn't block out the world any more, no matter what I did and no matter what I took. No matter who I was."

Craven put down his cup and said, with a tired look, "When I was twenty-seven I had two sons and was a year off getting a divorce. I never saw it coming. You think everything will stay the same. That you'll look like that, and be that same person you were when you were twenty-one forever. You just don't. We get older and change. Thing is, Jim, you're not dealing in reality, being a pop star, sunshine."

He picked up Jim's file and took out a photo of Jim from a *Weekly Music Express* clipping, recreating a topless Christ pose.

"Who has that kind of picture of themselves in their photo album, eh? And just think what you'd look like if we took the picture now." Craven looked down at Jim's stomach hanging over his belt. "Welcome to the real world. This is the real world now, son."

"Is it? Is that what it is? This whole situation is the weirdest thing that's ever happened to me."

Jim filled out papers to say he was alive and was informed that he should go back to The Railway Hotel "like nothing had happened". When Beatsy called he was to ring the station as soon as he could with the venue details. So as not to block his mobile from Beatsy, he was allowed to contact Lulu from the phone in the hallway outside his cell. Green sat on a chair opposite, watching him.

No reply.

Green allowed him one more call. He tapped in Lulu's mother's home number.

"Hello? Is –"

"Is that Jim?"

"Yes, hello, Mrs –"

"Jim. I'm sorry, love, but…"

"But what? Is she okay?"

"She isn't here at the moment."

"Where is she? When did she leave? Is she okay?" He spat out his words; couldn't help but sound desperate.

"Yes… yes, she's fine. But she told me she didn't want to speak to you. I'm sorry, but she wants me to hang up now. Sorry, love…"

"Hey!" he shouted. "I respect that. One more thing, Mrs Killshore. Don't let her go back into town…"

Mrs Killshore had hung up.

Jim nodded to Green, pleased enough that Lulu was safe, but was aching inside that she wouldn't speak to him.

On his way out into the reception, Jim noticed Craven walking back to his office.

"Did you find any other evidence at Burt's house, you know, of who could have killed him." Jim said.

Craven turned and leant his large frame against the shiny wall. "Just the shells from the weapon…"

Jim sniffed, gave a brief nod of acknowledgement and pivoted on his left foot for the door.

"Oh, Mr Vale, I suppose you know about the lab?"

Jim carried around full circle, facing Craven again.

"Lab?"

"Yes, in the spare room at the top of the house?"

"No…"

"Really?" Craven said with a disbelieving smirk.

"No, really, what lab?"

Craven stood upright and walked back into the reception.

"He was gathering equipment so he could make drugs in

136

big batches. We think it may have been crack."

"He told me I couldn't stay there because he was turning it into an observatory for his telescope."

"If I've learnt anything it's that you don't trust dealers and addicts. And where money is concerned, friendships dissolve… Remember, call us when you hear from Beatsy."

Craven turned and lumbered slowly down to his office, blocking out light, almost filling the corridor.

Jim made it halfway across the room before his phone rang. He pulled it out. Craven came back down the hallway. Jim checked the caller ID and nodded at Craven.

"Jim, yeah?" the voice said.

"Is this Beatsy?"

"Yeah, yeah. Listen, I want to talk to you. Business."

"Business? I don't know anything about business."

"You do. You do. My business. "

"Er…"

Jim looked over his shoulder. Craven nodded.

"Okay then. Let's talk."

"I'll get one of my boys to pick you up. Ten minutes. Where are you?"

Jim's eye began to twitch. "I'm busy at the moment –"

"Around seven o'clock outside The Railway Hotel. See you then."

The line went dead. So much for negotiation.

Jim looked round at Craven.

"He wants to pick me up outside The Railway Hotel at seven."

" Right. You'd better sit down here for a while. I've got a few things to sort out…"

A crumpled-looking Inspector Craven paced around his office, picking up various official-looking documents. He pulled a pile of notes from a cabinet that had a miniature white plastic Christmas tree on the top of it, and plonked the files on his desk.

"Jim…" Craven sat down. " So this is the plan. I'll have unmarked cars at the top of Railway Street, and one round the corner that will follow you at a distance. When we know your whereabouts, we'll send in backup."

Jim dug his nails into his left hand and began to scratch.

"Think what you will be achieving, Mr Vale. You'll be helping bring down a significant figure in Birmingham drug trafficking and opening us up to a very influential gang."

"So they'll follow the car, then send back up?"

"That's correct."

Jim felt a cold breeze from the open window behind Craven. "Inspector? Do you think I can get a bullet-proof vest?" he said, sinking his face deeper down into the padded collar of his coat.

Chapter 17

Jim stood outside The Railway Hotel in thin, drizzling rain, looking casually up and down the street as if he was waiting for a date.

Craven had suggested that it may be best for him not to wear a bullet-proof vest – if Beatsy clocked it, he would really risk getting shot. He decided to leave it off and hope for the best.

Jim wiped the rain from his stubbly head with one hand and with the other squeezed the bag of coke in his trouser pocket.

From behind him a car horn sounded. Jim turned to see a black Vauxhall Cavalier, the top half of the windscreen covered in a shading film obscuring the face of the driver, pull up to the curb.

He walked to the car, giving a cheery smile – trying to assure the people in the front seats, as much as himself, that everything was fine. He neared the driver's side. Within seconds a man with a cap pulled low over his face jumped out from the car, grabbed him and bungled him into the back seat. A sweet, grassy reek of dope clothed the air. The wheels spun, the force of the car's acceleration pushed him backward and a bag was pulled over his head. It smelt of soil and was drawn in by string that cut into his neck. He was squashed in between two large men, his shoulders pressing against their thick and solid arms. He felt his stomach twist and had the urge to shit.

No one spoke.

He hoped they hadn't noticed the blue Volvo and the black Escort parked up the road that were now, hopefully, following them.

His mouth was sticky and he couldn't swallow.

"Do I need this mask on, lads?" Jim said.

There was no reply.

A click of a switch. Bass exploded behind him from a speaker in the boot. The back seat buzzed. Then one of the men pushed Jim's head forward and held it down for the rest of the journey.

After what felt like ten minutes the car slowed and came to a halt.

Jim was grabbed by the arm, pulled across the seat and out the door.

Someone took the bag roughly off his head.

He squinted. His eyes ached as the landscape slowly sharpened around him. He was in a car park looking up at four grey, pebble-dashed tower blocks. Honey-yellow street lights around the estate glowed misty in the evening dark. Between two of the tower blocks was a playground lit up by floodlights and surrounded by a metal cross-wire fence.

He heard the car drive off behind him.

"Follow me."

Jim flicked his head to the right to see a tall and heavy-set kid, early twenties, dressed in a silver tracksuit with sky-blue piping running down the arms and legs. His head was square, his face was plump and he had an elaborate swirling pattern cut into his hair just above where his wide neck began.

"I'm Jim."

"Cheeks," said the kid in a sloppy baritone.

Jim looked around – no backup and no sign of the unmarked cars – but the playground was next to the main road and the exit came out on to a car park, so Craven could still get to him. The playground was empty but for someone sitting on a swing in the activity section. Jim saw purple-gloved hands held up on the chains, a cigarette in his mouth. He wore a white, high-fronted baseball cap perched on the back of his head, a black suit jacket and a pair of baggy stonewashed jeans. A boy at first glance, maybe thirteen, rocking back and forward, big white trainers stuck to the ground.

Cheeks remained silent at the gates as Jim walked over. Beatsy stood up and threw his cigarette on the floor. He straightened his sleeves and began to walk towards Jim. His face was long, his eyes large and sleepy. An unlit cigarette rested behind a small ear curled down by the cap.

"Hey…" Beatsy said and gave Jim a look that straddled menace and indifference.

Jim glanced at the road – still no police cars.

"Hey…" Jim said, making his voice deep and laconic. He sniffed and looked away, holding his cool. He was Robbie Johnson again, hard as fuck drug dealer.

Beatsy turned and walked towards the gate at the far end of the playground. "This way… this way."

Jim looked back. Cheeks was standing with a few small kids, no older than nine or ten. Two older boys stood next to them surrounded in cigarette smoke and breath-steam, all of them staring at Jim.

"Yo! This way," Beatsy shouted.

The path led to another yard surround by low garages, the shutters all faded yellows and pinks. Beatsy approached one up the far end, pulled out a key from his jacket, jiggled it around in the lock and pushed the shutter up.

"Come on, I've not got all day."

Jim stopped and scanned the car park, then carried on. This could be it, he thought. This could be the end.

The door screeched down behind Jim, leaving them in pitch black.

There was a click, a buzzing sound.

A light came on.

"Welcome to my office. Take a seat."

Beatsy pointed to two upturned wooden containers. Jim sat down on one. The walls were covered with hip-hop posters: Wu-Tang Clan, Naughty by Nature, Cannibus, Ja Ru the Damager and plenty Jim didn't recognise – men with huge fur coats and diamond-rimmed sunglasses, a woman on each arm dressed in a skimpy pink bikini. On the left wall in the centre, over the top of the posters, there was a small print. Jim recognised it – *Starry Night* by Van Gogh. It was very quiet in there, and the smell of freshly smoked dope and damp clung to the walls.

Beatsy went over to a rusty cabinet and pulled out one of

the draws; it made a metallic popping sound as it slid out. He plunged both hands in, then turned, a large red folder stuffed with paper in his hand.

He concentrated on his trainers and said, "It's like this. I just wanted to show you where I'm coming from with this idea, you know. Me and Burt, we did business together…"

Jim decompressed a little as Beatsy sat down on one of the boxes, still not looking him in the eye. He opened the folder and passed it over to Jim, his head nodding slightly.

"Have a look."

Jim flicked through the pages – drawings of what looked like computer game characters drawn in pencil. Ghetto kids bulked up with robotic attachments on their legs, some with machine guns for arms. Gold teeth, thick necks and cartoon-wide biceps. Their names were written in bold gothic typefaces underneath: *Sirius Street Killa*, *Ghost Face Taker*, *Da' Sweet Revenger*.

"Where did you learn to draw?" Jim said, head down, looking at the page.

"Learn? I could always draw. Never went to college."

"Why, man?"

Beatsy tutted and shook his head.

Jim turned to the last page. This one was painted with great detail and in vibrant reds and yellows – a man dressed in a long fur coat, like the rappers on the posters. The face looked like Beatsy's; the name underneath said *Daddy Mac*. A machine gun pointed at the temple of a dead man and a buxom girl dressed in nothing but an orange thong was on *Daddy Mac*'s other arm.

Just then Jim felt something cold and hard gouging into the top of his head.

"Look up. No sudden shit," said Beatsy.

Jim felt the pressure drop from his skull and he slowly looked up.

The gun slid down his forehead and over his nose.

"Open wide."

Jim opened his mouth a little. Beatsy twisted the gun sideways and pushed it into the back of Jim's mouth. Jim breathed faster – in and out through his nose; the taste of metal on his tongue, the gun barrel blocking his airway.

"Raise your hands."

Jim took his hands off the folder.

"Slowly…" Beatsy's eyes hardened and he rattled the gun quickly from side to side over Jim's teeth.

Jim lifted his arms and placed them on his head.

"Right. Let's get this straight. *Do not*. I repeat: *do not* fuck me about," Beasty said calmly.

A gargle came from Jim's throat over the nub of the gun. "Shut up!" Beasty's voice exploded. "I'm not fuckin' asking ya, I'm telling ya. Stand up… Stand up now!"

Jim stood up, his hands on his head touching the rusty roof, shards crumbling over him.

With his free hand Beatsy pulled open Jim's coat and searched the pockets. He took the bag of cocaine, all the while not breaking his glare. He patted down Jim's legs, chest, crotch and backside. Then he took the gun out of Jim's mouth and stood back. His mouth closed, Beatsy slid his tongue up over his top teeth and narrowed his eyes.

"I don't know nothing about ya. Only what Burt said. Had a hit song or somfin'?"

Jim nodded.

Beatsy brought the gun down by his leg and shrugged.

"That was just a little somfin' to show you I'm serious."

"I believe you…" Jim swallowed. "I just don't understand why you're showing me the pictures…"

"You see. Out there? This shithole? I'm getting out, man. You see the players round here? All they got is other players round here, ya get me? Or they all want to be rappers. Think they're fucking something special, man." He dropped his head to the side and shook it in despair. "No offence… but music's a mug's game, innit?"

"Well…"

"My thing is wedge, you get me?" Beatsy strode over to the metal cabinet and started to push it, bumping and squeaking, to the wall. He bent down and looked over at Jim. "You got to have a road out, you understand? The other gangs? They don't know they're even on a road. They're stuck on some fuckin' island going round and round."

He pulled a rotten plank of wood up from the floor, dipped his hand down into the cavity. He brought out a carrier bag, put the cocaine into it and placed it back under the floorboards.

"The gangs, right – there's a Jamaican term, right. Crabs in a barrel?"

"Go on…" Jim said.

"Well, when you go fishing for crabs, when you catch them you throw all your crabs into a barrel and some of the crabs try to get out –"

Jim nodded.

"They try to climb over the other crabs and up to the lid of the barrel. But the crabs at the bottom, every time they see one of the other crabs reaching the lip, trying to escape, they lift a claw and pull it back down with the rest of them. So you understand me now? When you're in a gang, it's like they're your family, innit. And they don't want you to leave."

"I know a bit about that myself…" Jim held his aching jaw and wobbled it back and forth, wincing.

"Right. Right. The thing is, I got plans to move on, man… The drawings are characters I have for a computer game idea – 'Ghetto Life'. You start young at the bottom, right? Get in a gang, do some drops, then you work your way up. Steal a car, break-ins, deal a few class B's. All the time you're trying to stay alive, protect your crew *and* make sure you mum's not mad at you and you don't get slapped when you get back late."

Jim nodded along.

"Then, if you pass that, you work your way up more shit for the gang and become head gangster. Top dog, man. Then it's bigger deals. Sortin' out rival gangs. Shoot-outs. If you fail, you have to go through the whole legal shit, do P and all that. I got it all planed out. Even got sequels, like when you're head of the gang you go on and be a club promoter or a rap star.

'I want you to take me to see Jacob Little. I want to tell him about my idea, sell it, develop it. I'm sick of this bullshit, too old for it now. Got a kid, ya get me? She's not going through this."

Beatsy rubbed his chin with his long, bony fingers and

looked away at the posters. "On my road, things that get in the way get knocked off it. You know your mate? He thought the same. Hate to say it, in the end, some point Burt would've knocked you off too. He was in way too deep. Understand? He told me that you were going to bring in shitloads of cash from record producers and all that. But it never happened, did it?"

"That's why you killed him? 'Cause he was in the way, on your road? You only had to wait a couple of hours, you would have your –"

"Killed him? No. No. I didn't kill him," Beatsy said through a sly smile, looking at his gun.

Jim cocked his head, not believing a word. "Who did then?"

"You don't want to know. Best just to keep out and calm down, innit…"

"No, you better tell me."

Beatsy stood up straight, scratching his head with the gun.

"Yeah? What you going to do if I don't?" He shrugged and blew a laugh down his nose and turned back to his bag.

"It's not me you got to be worried about…"

Beatsy turned. His mouth opened a little, his eyes narrowed and he shook his head. "What have you done, Jim? You haven't done something stupid, have ya?"

Jim searched the floor for an answer. He sat down on his box, knowing he had nothing and everything to lose.

"Sit down, man. I can help you." He pointed to the other crate.

Beatsy held up his gun with both hands, flicked off the safety catch and pointed it down at Jim's head.

"Speak."

"I was brought in by the police early this morning. They spoke to… you know Stuart, Burt's flatmate? He tried to pin Burt's shooting on me, but as you can see, I'm a lover not a fighter." Jim smiled.

"Keep talking!" Beatsy shouted, his eyes burning into Jim's, still holding the gun at his face.

"Stuart mentioned you, and because of Burt not paying

you back, it was an obvious motive… that you'd kill him."

Beatsy's nose twitched and he began grinding his teeth.

"They think you did it and they're going to be here any minute."

Jim waited for the gun to crack – white-hot death from a bullet. Beatsy didn't blink. He remained frozen in the same position.

"They gave me coke so that I could set you up, so they can bring you in legit, like. Please, man … just don't do anything you may regret. If you didn't do it, you got nothing to worry about. If it's about you getting out of here…"

"Fucking bastards," Beatsy said, then looked around the room, as if searching for a way to escape.

"Beatsy. If it wasn't you then who was it? 'Cause you want to get your story sorted."

Beatsy's head bobbed up and down and a hard, sickly smile emerged. "It's the fucking Krayzz man. Fucking Phaser."

"Why would The Krayzz shoot him? What's it got to do with them?"

"'Cause its two birds with one stone, innit. Burt was selling his stuff real low, man, low price, ya get me? Undercutting The Krayzz, taking their business. And for me? Burt owed me money. Money that I needed to get the fuck out, man. Someone I want to do business with in the future. Crabs in a barrel. Spite, man. Fucking spite."

The shutter rattled with a knock.

Beatsy looked coldly at Jim.

Jim felt his heart stop for a moment.

Beatsy flicked his head towards the shutter, gesturing for him to speak.

"Yeah?" Jim shouted.

"Yo, it's Cheeks, man. Can I come in? It's cold out here, ya know…"

"Cheeks. This is Jim… you by yourself?"

There was a pause.

"Er, yeah, come on. Is Beats there? It's fucking cold, man."

Beatsy lowered his gun. His shoulders dropped, and he exhaled and sucked his teeth.

Jim stood up and walked to the garage door. He put his hand on the handle and looked back at Beatsy. "One more thing. My girlfriend has nothing to do with this. Nothing. So leave her out of it. Okay?"

Beatsy gave a short nod.

Jim pushed up the shutter.

Blinding white light flooded the garage.

A cacophony of "Don't move!" and "Put the gun down!"

Jim lifted his hand to shade his eyes and saw Cheeks in handcuffs next to Green and Doyle. Behind them stood six police officers: three with guns held out in front of their chests ready to fire and three holding up large torches.

"Sorry, man, they just… you know… I'm sorry, blood," Cheeks said to his feet.

Jim held up his hands and walked forwards slowly.

"It's okay… don't shoot." He turned to Beatsy. "Just tell 'um what you told me. Okay, Beatsy?"

Beatsy's head had dropped and he was staring at the hole in the floorboard.

"Jim? All good?" Craven said firmly.

Jim took off his coat. He wanted to take off everything and feel light, weightless – float off over the flats.

"Oh, just great, thanks, Inspector," he said, walking out behind the torches.

Craven nodded and spoke over his shoulder: "Okay, lads."

Three of the officers shuffled forwards into the garage, guns up, trained on Beatsy.

"You can put them down. I'm not doing any fin' stoopid."

Jim walked off towards the police van with Sergeant Doyle. He heard a dull thud and turned back to the garage.

"Hey!" Beatsy shouted.

One of the officers had knocked Beatsy's portfolio off the top of the box onto the floor.

"Watch my fucking drawings, man. Swear to God…"

Chapter 18

Jim scanned the white ceiling in the cell and counted the number of hardened spit-balls that dotted its surface. He wondered about all the people who had been held there, waiting to know their fate. The possibility that the outcome could be something horrific, he knew now, was never an inch away from the possibility of freedom. His stomach growled for food and he needed a cigarette. Or preferably a tidal wave of JD to crash him onto a warmer shore.

When Sergeant Doyle opened the cell door he couldn't tell whether he'd been there for six hours or fifteen hours. Doyle and Green stood either side of him and walked Jim down the corridor into the interrogation room without saying a word.

Under a band of blue cigarette smoke, delicately scratching his head through his thinning hair, Craven was hunched over a stack of files. Doyle left without saying a word. Green pulled up a chair next to Craven.

After a moment Craven pushed the files away on the desk and sat up. His eyes were watery behind square, gold-rimmed glasses.

"Mr Vale." He smiled.

"You look how I feel," Jim said.

Craven winked, placed an ashtray on the yellow notepad in front of him, keeping his attention on Jim all the while.

"We've had a word with Mr Beatsy Lewis, Jim. He's been very helpful, given us a few leads, opened up a few locked doors. We were shocked." Craven turned to Green. "Weren't we, Sergeant…"

Green nodded.

"I sensed something different about him, something that a lot of the kids who come in here don't usually show," Craven leaned forward . "Fear," he said. "It seems Beatsy's had enough.

Says he can't hack it any more. Wants us to call him by his real name now, Shaun. He says he's too old. He's twenty-seven…" Craven raised an eyebrow. "Desperate to get out of the situation that he put himself in. He won't say it, but this type of behaviour – admitting he was at fault, dumping his street name for his real one – classic symptoms of a scared man trying to get out. Sound familiar? Maybe you were onto something, Jim Vale."

Craven took a box of Embassy from his pocket and pulled out a cigarette.

"He's denying all charges of murder. Says he can prove he was with the mother of his child at the time. We've had conformation on that. His forensics looked clean as a whistle, too. He's saying it's Phaser from his old gang who shot Burt. Apart from the fact that Phaser is taking out every dealer in the city, Beatsy reckons that Burt's death was a setup, to punish him for leaving The Krayzz and stopping any future business."

Craven looked over to Jim for an answer.

"Why would Beatsy lie to me? If it's all about intimidation, surely he'd tell me he'd slaughtered all of them," Jim said.

"Right," Craven said, rolling the cigarette between his fingers and placing it down on the table. "Fear for their life, of poverty, of being trapped forever in a cycle of destruction, drives people to do things that they never even considered before. Dangerous things. In this case, upping and leaving a world that they've profited from. Even if it means they may get hurt somewhere down the line."

"I can't disagree with that," Jim said.

"We've passed Beatsy an offer. He wants to go clean. He's going to work with us. Do a deal. Get some of the main players," Craven said, putting the cigarette on the table and rolling it towards Jim. "So we need you to help us again."

Jim looked down at the cigarette and shook his head. He could almost feel the hit of nicotine collapse those tense muscles around his neck. Eyes getting heavy, he squinted over at Craven.

"Come on. I thought that was it. That it was over. I was

free to go. I've risked my life enough."

Craven sniffed and looked at Green, then back at Jim.

"According to Beatsy, that internet brat Jacob Little is having a big Millennium party. Beatsy said you'd introduce him to Jacob so he could offer his game as a new business deal."

"He also said that The Krayzz will be attending," Green said. "There are more and more younger splinter gangs in the city now. Popping up, taking their business. Recently Phaser and The Krayzz have gone from being a medium-level gang to a big presence, taking over a lot of the business from the other gangs. Phaser wants Beatsy back in the gang. If they had Beatsy, they'd be more powerful than ever."

Jim, desperate to scratch his scabs and aching to sleep, picked up the cigarette, which glowed white under the strip lights. "What if I don't want to? Haven't I done my bit? Beatsy could have blown my fucking head off back there…" He patted around the table looking for the lighter.

"Jim, have you considered how this all looks?" Craven leaned back in his chair.

"All what looks like?"

"You wouldn't have read today's papers, but the press reckon you're involved in dealing drugs. They're saying that you could have killed your best friend. Killed him? I'm no genius, but it doesn't look good, does it? I mean, in the eyes of the public, being involved in a murder case? There's also a rumour floating around that your disappearance was all a scam to get you in the papers." Craven sniffed and looked at Green. "It's not really a good thing to waste the police's time. You can be prosecuted for that. And if your fans found out that you lied to them… Not cool, Jimmy. We can turn this around for you."

Craven pulled a lighter from his pocket and slid it up and down between his fingers, his eyes locked on Jim's.

Jim felt the cigarette filter, round and firm, between his lips.

"What will happen to Beatsy?"

Green stood up and stretched. "He'll be going down for stolen goods, maybe possession," he said, loosening his shoulders back into position. "But he won't be going down half as long as he would've done."

"When he gets out he'll be seen as a snitch. What about his daughter?" Jim said.

"All being well, we'll relocate him."

"Inspector, I don't care at all what the press say, or what anyone says any more..." Jim held out his hand to Craven. "I'll call Jacob and set up the meeting. But that's it. I just want the person who killed Burt brought in."

A smile slowly rose on Craven's craggy face and he slapped the lighter into Jim's hot palm.

Green pulled out Jim's mobile from his jacket pocket and placed it carefully in front of Jim. Jim found Jacob's number and punched 'Call' with his thumb.

After four rings, Jacob answered.

"What you want, blood?"

Jim heard gunfire rattling off and screams.

"Jacob, it's Burt's lackey? Remember me? I brought around the stash for your party."

"Yeah, yeah, I know. Quick. I'm halfway through the last level of a Japanese prisoner of war game. I'm nearly out of there..."

"It's about the Millennium party."

"Right, yeah, you coming? Oh, shit, I heard what happened to Burt, man. Sorry, blood, the kid got burned, man. R.I.P. Got ya!"

The screams got louder, so Jim spoke louder.

"Thanks... Listen. I'm still coming. I just need –"

There was a bassy explosion on the end of the line.

"Yes!" Jacob whooped.

"I've got someone who wants to meet you as well. Is that okay?" Jim said.

"At fuckin' last, man, I'm out of that fuckin' prison. Blew that fucker to smithereens..." The game's end of level music played, distorted by the volume. "What's that? Someone, to... yeah, fine. I'll sign a game for them, give them a T-shirt or something."

"Thanks, Jacob –"

"Listen, I thought I knew you when you came round. You can't play a player. I saw you on TV. You're Jimmy Tyrant. 'Snitches.' I fucking love Sizzle man's song – you're the singer. Die you fucker!" More screams and pleading from the characters in the game. "Easy. We can have the meeting, yeah, but you've got to sing 'Snitches' at some point. That tune is massive, man."

Jim dropped his head to the table. "Really, you don't want me sing that, Jacob. I mean –"

"No song, no meeting. Simple, blood."

Jim's throat felt dry at the thought of being on stage. He looked up to see Craven and Green looking at him.

"Okay, Jacob. For you, I'll do it."

"Wicked."

The line went dead. Jim put down the phone.

"Well?" Craven said.

"Looks like you'll get to hear me sing after all, Inspector."

Chapter 19

Jim leaned his body into the front door of the police station, near enough falling out onto the street.

"Mr Vale, I was wondering if I could talk to you about the killing of your friend, the drug dealer Marion Parker Baines, known as Burt?"

Jim turned around.

From around the side of the building a bright light was shone into his eyes, and then a microphone was pushed underneath his nose. It was being held by the local TV reporter Tulip Jones.

"No comment," Jim said and carried on down the street, his arms and legs seemingly full of lead and concrete. Tulip followed. Jim pushed the mic out of his face. Then, with a burst of energy, he paced forwards past the cameraman.

He heard a car slow down by the side of him.

"Jim! Hey, matey. It's Craig!"

Jim turned to see Craig Beakington through the wound-down window of a mustard Volvo estate crawling by the curb.

"Hop in. I'll give you a lift."

The cameraman was now walking at Jim's left-hand side; Tulip was just about to scoot in front of him.

"That would be good," Jim said.

Craig stopped and threw open the door. Jim hopped off the pavement and into the passenger's seat.

"Mr Vale, before you go, could you please say something about your role in all of this?" Tulip shouted after him.

Jim wound down the window as Craig pulled away fast from the curb. "None of this is what you think. Or what it seems…" he said, leaving Tulip holding out the mic as they sped off down onto the main road, onto the Queensway.

"You want to take a right, past the town hall."

"I know. I've been looking in every flea pit in the city for you," Craig said, and smiled.

Christmas traffic was slow across the city centre. The heat from the air-con mixed with the Brian Eno compilation Craig had slipped into the tape player worked like an opiate. Jim needed to sleep more than ever. He wondered whether a drink would sort it out; but he couldn't stomach one. Craven was right. He was getting older. Problems took a lot longer to fix. Alcohol only made him feel worse. His mornings were once again spent with the incomprehensible voices that came to him first when he'd drunk himself to sleep on the tour bus around Europe.

Craig pulled up outside the front door of The Railway Hotel and turned the engine off.

"Cheers, Craig. I'll see you around sometime."

Jim pushed opened the door and got out.

"You don't think I'm letting you get away that easily, do you, Jim?" Craig said, following him out onto the pavement.

Through the dimpled glass of the front door Jim could see the familiar, blurred figures of his band sitting around a table. He turned back onto the road. Craig stood right behind him, his arm outstretched, casually blocking the way onto the street.

"Look. It's a quick interview. Just to talk things over, the whole story of you being found. What the band think. This is a big deal, Jim. You're a big deal. The album is – it's genius. The most exciting thing to happen in music for years, mate. You've become a cult figure. The *Weekly Music Express* is fuckin' inundated with letters about you and your whereabouts every day... Come on. The papers sells shitloads 'cause of your disappearance. And you've sold a shitload 'cause of us. Please... I've been all over the shop looking for you. Do me and yourself a favour."

Craig was smiling but his eyebrows twitched with nervous aggression. "It's only an interview..." he said.

Jim sighed, turned and pushed open the door.

"Rock and Roll Christmas" played from the speakers. The

Tyrants were sitting around a table under the TV. Dennis was next to Dimpy, talking closely into his ear. Dimpy nodded along earnestly. In the corner, by the pool table, the rest of Dennis's crew threw Jim dead-eyed looks as he made his way over.

"Look who I've found!" Craig shouted, slapping Jim on the back.

Gary, Lon and Paulo looked towards him at the same time. Now he was nearer Jim could see that they were all wearing the same black-and-white chequered jackets, the same white shirt and the same skinny, black tie. They all had mop-top haircuts. They'd gone from The Stooges to Gerry and the Pacemakers in just over a month.

Each of them held on their laps a box wrapped in red Christmas paper with a sparkling green and silver bow on the top.

"Alright, mate!"

Gary stood up, trying to smile, holding his hand out to be shook. Jim ignored him and stood in front of them. Gary's nose was bent to the side, red and plump around the bridge. The black rings under his eyes were just about starting to disappear. Self-consciously, Gary lifted his hand to his face.

"No hard feelings, hey, mate. Looks like the karma police paid a visit to you 'en all." He pointed to Jim's nose.

Jim had forgotten about it since it had stopped hurting.

"A right pair of bruisers, eh…" Gary said with a big grin.

Jim remained silent. He felt his stomach rumble and suddenly felt a little nauseous.

"Jim, my son!"

Jim jerked around to be grabbed by Dimpy. His shiny, bald head, smelling of Brut aftershave, was wedged under Jim's nose as his ribs were crushed by Dimpy's bear-like grip. Dennis stood a few feet behind Dimpy. He nodded, gave a friendly wink and a thumbs-up.

"Thanks for getting your manager down here, mate! You did the right thing," Dennis said.

Dimpy pulled away and looked up with his wide, tooth-stuffed grin.

Jim's mouth began to water; he felt sweaty, shaky.

"The mid-week charts are all saying we're the Christmas number one! Nice one, Jimmy boy! We fuckin' did it."

Then the band had surrounded him, pushing their presents up to his face. Tony came over with a silver tray crammed with full glasses of champagne.

"The best Christmas ever, eh, Jimmy boy!" Dimpy plucked a glass from the tray and put it in Jim's hand.

The band all cheered.

"Get a shot of this, sunshine!" Dimpy shouted and a man at the bar with a camera slung around his neck came over and began taking shots.

"I forgive you, mate. Forget it, yeah? Just fucking smile, will ya? This is going to make us massive," Gary hissed into Jim's ear through a gritted smile. The camera flashed and kaleidoscopic blobs floated across Jim's vision.

Dimpy snatched Jim's glass away and Gary brought over his big gift and pushed it into Jim's stomach. Jim grabbed it with both hands. It was light. Jim shook it. It was empty.

The camera flashed again.

Jim caught sight of Paulo forcing a pleading smile. His jacket was pulled tightly around his shoulders, the sleeves of it falling too short on his wrists.

Jim turned back to the camera and felt the room shudder. He couldn't hold it any more. His stomach flinched, he lurched forwards and vomit sprayed from his mouth, splattering onto Gary's shoes.

"Wooh! You okay, matey?" Craig shouted; then Jim heard him say into the cameraman's ear, "Did you get that?"

"Doesn't matter, doesn't matter, it's just a bit of sick... Paulo, could you go and get me a towel?" Gary said, looking down at his shoes. "We used to get drunk all the time together, eh, mate, and we were always sick! Remember those days, mate? Like brothers!"

Jim looked up and wiped his mouth. "Don't, Paulo, don't do it. Don't listen to him. He can get it himself."

But Paulo was already on his way.

Gary turned to Craig, shrugged his shoulders, then patted

Jim on the back. "Get it all out, mate. Feel free to go again. Come on…"

Jim stood upright, wiped his mouth with the sleeve of his Puffa jacket and looked Gary in the eye.

"Why are you here? I thought I was no longer a member of The Tyrants. I've been thrown out. Too mentally unstable…"

"No, ha! No, Jim," Dimpy said from behind him. "That's why we're here. We want to ask you to come back. Re-join the band."

"After what you've made me do? Burt's fucking dead, Dimp. Did you know that? He's dead… You don't care whose life is pushed around and ripped open. Or even if they die. As long as you get paid. Do you?"

Jim turned to the band. Lon's head was down, his hair like a sheet shielding him from the conversation. Gary's smile had gone and he was giving Jim a blank stare.

"I can't believe the amount of humiliation you'll put yourself through to sell a few records. I used to believe you, Gary, that it was all about the music and us, as a group. Us against them. That we'd never sell out. I believed you when you said I could sing, that you thought I could be a great singer. That we were friends… What's this you're wearing? Look at you! You look like a fucking barber shop quartet, man. You used to have at least a little bit of dignity. And, Lon? Have you got fake tan on?"

Lonny mumbled something through his hair.

"What?"

"He said it's because… we're having our photo taken," Gary said, starting the sentence with a sense of conviction then letting it peter out near the end as he realised the absurdity of his words.

The gents' door squeaked open and Paulo walked out holding a toilet roll.

"Paulo, what do you think?"

"About what, Jim?"

"About this ridiculous setup. Those stupid clothes, and the fact that one minute I'm dropped like I'm a rabid dog, the next you want me back and want to pet me like a puppy or something… What happened to friendship?"

Paulo was gripping the toilet roll to his chest with both hands now. He glanced at Dimpy, then slowly around to Jim.

"Well… I think you should come back, mate. Like the old times."

Jim dropped his head and remembered the early days, the feeling that they were all connected. His new family – a family that would listen to him; one that told him anything was possible and that together they were greater than every other band, which deep down they all knew was based only on the fear that they weren't. He recalled the manic look on the A&R man's face, flushed with Burt's coke, and the realisation that at that moment he was signing away his life, and his dreams, on the dotted line to a complete stranger…

"Paulo, out of this lot you know you're the only one I'd trust. And you're a loyal friend to them. I can see what you're doing. You're a nice guy. Too fuckin' nice. We can't go back to how it was before. Only forward. How can you even think that it's all going be okay again?… I wouldn't want to come back to the band. I don't know if I could; I'm not the same person I was back then."

Paulo looked at Jim like he'd betrayed him..

"It's like we've been lured in by this beautiful mirage, where there'd be fame, women, fucking fortune, immortality – God knows what. But really we wanted to be someone else. All we became was just another product. I thought I'd become a commodity when we signed our deal. But now I know, Gary: you always saw me as a commodity, something to get you famous."

Gary said nothing, but Jim could see his chest rising up and down, trying to quell his anger. Craig chewed on his pen, his smile still in place, but his eyebrows had dropped and he looked embarrassed.

"Jim, I think you're going a little over the top here, mate. Think about what you're saying," Dimpy said with a crazed smile to Craig.

"Gary? You'll forgive me for punching you? Craig, did he tell you why I punched him? Did he tell you that I overheard him and Dimpy talking about having me replaced by Sammy from The Mirrors? The man who also took my girlfriend? This was after 'Tell Me Reasons', when Bix became interested in me. My dad's gone. My mum's slowly going crazy. Lulu doesn't want to know me. The record's hit the fucking fan… And you wonder why I acted the way I did? Congratulations, Gary, you got what you wanted. You used me until I was empty then chucked me out… I had nothing, man. Do you understand now?"

Jim walked away from them and up the stairs. Halfway up the first flight he turned and looked down.

"So the answer's no. I'm not coming back. Threaten me with what you like, Dimp. I don't care. You can't play me around like that anymore. I know what's right now. And I've got more important things to do… Way more important things to do."

Chapter 20

On the morning of Christmas Eve Jim slid the side panel off the bath in his room at The Railway Hotel and was relieved to see that the money was still there. He paid Tony off, wished him a happy Christmas and was told he could come back and stay any time he liked. He negotiated his way through the tightly packed crowds of last-minute shoppers on New Street, past the carol singers outside St Philip's Cathedral and down to the police station, where he asked to see Sergeant Green about Burt's old Escort. It was clean of any evidence, and because he would need it for the Millennium party, Sergeant Green gave him the keys and took him down to the compound. Jim signed a form, hopped in the driver's seat, turned the key and headed out on to the road. He wound down the window, flicked on the radio and turned the volume up as loud as it would go, so whatever Christmas tune playing became distorted and unrecognisable. Now it was too loud and too cold to think, but anticipation sat lodged like a hot stone in his gut. To avoid traffic he drove down back streets out of the city, onto the M5, to Worcester.

"Lu?"

"What do you want?"

"Thank God you answered."

"What do you want, Jim?"

"Merry Christmas." He smiled.

"Is that it? Is that what you rang for?"

"No. Lu…" Jim swallowed, trying to stop his voice from cracking. "Erm, can I see you…"

Lulu paused.

"Well, I'm at my mum's, and its Christmas, so, you know… Where are you?"

"I'm outside your mum's house."

Jim looked up at the window of the squat thatched cottage. Lulu seemed to materialise in the frame. Her hair was down and falling over the shoulders of a black Alice Cooper T-shirt. She was looking at him now. He saw her lips move and a second later the phone caught up.

"I'll be down in five," she said, and walked away from the window.

Lulu let him in and he followed her down the hall into the kitchen. It was warm and smelt of coffee and slow-cooked meat. He sat down in a pine chair at the oak dining table that took up most of the room. Ernest, Lulu's St Bernard, pushed his large, heavy head onto Jim's lap and Lulu tutted. She put a mug in front of Jim, then grabbed the dog's thick brown leather collar, pulled him away, and sat in the chair opposite Jim.

"I was worried about what might have happened to you... I hadn't heard from you," he said.

"I was doing some thinking."

From the window motes of dust fell lazily through the shaft of late autumn sun across the table between them.

"So did you think about us? I mean, did you think about making the album?"

Lulu pulled a black wing of hair back from her eyes.

"Do you know how difficult this has all been, Jim? Do you know? After you left, for a while I found it difficult to trust anyone. I was permanently confused about everything."

He nodded.

"The Girlies were going nowhere and you were drinking too much, so we started to argue. When you were drunk, you would never listen. Never. I know I threw you out , but it was meant to be a warning – that you'd lose me if you didn't stop trying to kill yourself. I was angry. You seemed to be spinning more and more out of control... Then I kept seeing you in the music press and wondering why you'd just upped and left without even a fucking note to say when, or if, you would be back. But most of all, I bloody missed you."

Lulu rested her head on her hands, covering her eyes and

made a loud humming noise. Eventually Jim saw the corners of her pursed mouth loosen. She took her hands from her face.

"I had to drink to get on stage and be Jimmy Tyrant. Without it, I wouldn't have been able to talk to you – me, a scrawny, council house, country bumpkin loser going out with a girl like you."

Lulu wiped her eyes and shook her head.

"Every man or woman you spoke to, I was jealous of. I was scared to lose you."

"Jim… Oh, that's so wrong. That's so not the case."

They sat in silence for a while, looking at the same spot of light in the middle of the table. Then, slowly, Lulu reached across and placed her hand over Jim's scabbed and scarred fingers.

"So, do you think we can make this album together… is it yes or no, Lu? I need to know for sure."

"Having this time out to think about everything… I mean your lyrics, my music – there's no denying, it does work… But it won't be like before, Jim."

"It can't be," Jim said.

Lulu began to smile. Jim stood up, a storm of joy in his belly. He leant over the table, cupped his hand around her neck and kissed her forehead.

"Hey!" she said fussily.

"You won't regret it, Lu. It'll be the best thing we've done. Bix is a freekin' genius."

Lulu pushed Jim away, straightened her hair and dropped her grin. "Okay. Okay. Don't carried away. We have to finish writing the songs first. When is it we go?"

Jim sat back down, his heart drumming, bobbing his head, trying to remember what Bix had said.

"A week or so after New Year's. A week before my twenty-eighth."

"Perfect."

"There's another thing. A favour. I need somewhere to stay for a while."

Jim sipped his tea, and then he told her about getting

caught by the police, singing at the Millennium party and having to introduce Beatsy to Jacob Little.

After he finished he could see that she was still unsure.

"Phaser shot Burt. He's trying to take out all the other gangs, take over the drugs in the city. And because I'm associated with Burt, I'll have to stay out of town till after New Year's. And you're best staying out the way too."

She puffed her cheeks, exhaled loudly and looked away from him. For a moment he thought she may cry.

"Fine. I'll have to ask Mum and Allen. They're going to Spain on Boxing Day... You'll have to stay in the spare room."

Jim smiled, shoulders loosening with relief.

"Thanks, Lu. Seriously."

She sipped her coffee, placed her head on her folded arms and watched as Ernest stood up wearily and waddled out the room.

That evening Lulu's mother, Harriet, cooked a ham; it glistened, golden under the dim lights of the kitchen. Lulu's stepfather Allen – his long, thin, white hair swept back, his blue-and-white-striped shirt collar open – poured a deep ruby-coloured wine into a crystal glass in front of Jim and told him it was "a very good Rioja". Lulu looked up at him over her meal and raised her eyebrow. Jim drank one glass, finished his meal and ate cheese and biscuits with Allen in the lounge.

Full and exhausted, that night Jim got into the single bed in the spare room and slept a deep and imageless sleep.

On Christmas Day, along with the turkey Harriet served lime pickle, a tradition that had stuck when Lulu's Indian-born father, who had died when she was twelve, insisted on it one year to give the turkey "a bit more of a kick". Jim phoned the halfway house and was told that his mother was having her Christmas meal with the other residents. She was doing well and he was more than welcome to visit. But Jim felt anxious about having to tell her about getting arrested and the Millennium party and politely declined.

Boxing Day morning, Jim and Lulu waved Harriett and

Allen off from the driveway. Over the next three days they woke late, had breakfast, then worked hard on the songs until well into the evening. As they discussed chord changes and harmonies Jim tried to make eye contact, but Lulu always managed to be concerned with something more important in the score. He could sense she was still not sure that she had made the right choice. On tea breaks and when making dinner she moved around him in the kitchen as if he had a terrible cold that she was afraid she may catch.

But on the third night, after finishing three arrangements, a few B-side ideas and a turkey curry that Lulu had knocked up, they shared two bottles of Rioja from Allen's wine rack and ended up in Lulu's bed. Afterwards Jim dug out Nick Drakes' "Bryter Layter" album from Lulu's record collection. He placed it on her stereo that she'd had since she was a teenager and dropped the needle on "Northern Sky". He spooned up beside her and let his hand slip down over her small, soft belly. He felt so far away from the confusion that had engulfed his life over the last year, and for the rest of the night she slept in the nook of his arms. It was natural, warm, still. Even with this feeling, he could not sleep. He lay staring at the ceiling. On the city streets Jim would be seen as heir to Burt's business; Phaser's last standing competition, and therefore the next hit for The Krayzz. Going to the same party as The Krayzz was a suicide mission. To think, just a month ago he had wanted to end it all, would have welcomed, even willed, a bullet to hit him – and now, more than anything, he wanted to live.

Chapter 21

Face clean-shaven, head now covered in dark fuzz and dressed in his leather jacket and jeans that were a bit tight, Jim handed over the tickets to a man with a Marc Bolan hairdo and a lazy eye who was sitting in the lodge at the gates to Jacob Little's house.

Bowls full of brassy flames held up by silver poles lined the road through the wood leading to the house. As he pulled the car onto the drive a dilapidated coach painted pink with yellow flowers trundled off to the left towards a huge bonfire that was letting off wriggling flames into the warped night sky. There was a free-standing stage, a rainbow of light pouring from its mouth. On the opposite side of the field a large white-framed Ferris wheel was turning unhurriedly, the cabins glowing like gold baubles. Jim had the urge to stop the car and go evacuate his guts under a tree.

He parked in front of the house, which was surrounded by even more bowls of fire, making it shimmer a tropical shade of orange. He wiped his hands on his thighs, sweat stinging the cracks in his fingers, then opened the door with a rusty creak.

A tall, thin man with long, black hair wearing a red velvet jacket with nothing on underneath it and skin-tight jeans came down the steps of the house towards Jim. The expression on the man's arrow-shaped face was serious as he pointed at the car.

"Yer can't park there, pal, you know that," he said in a strong Mancunian accent.

"I'm here to see Jacob? I'm Jim Vale."

The man gave a sly, coke-induced pout and nodded, wide-eyed, then bobbed up and down and said in a loud whisper, "Nearly didn't recognise yer, Jim! You're a fuckin' legend, man!"

He held out his hand, and when Jim shook it, he pulled him in and hugged him. "He said you were coming, but I thought the fuckin' pigs would have you in the fuckin' nick, kid. Or you'd be in yer cave in France or whatever. You're a fuckin' outlaw, man. Ha, ha! This way, geezer."

Jim followed the man into the vast hallway of the house. A hip-hop song he'd never heard before was playing loud over a PA setup in the lounge. Spotlights were angled at the ceiling. Jacob's mural above glowed and the scene seemed more vivid than before.

"There's someone who's coming along with me to see Jacob…"

The man started up the left-hand staircase. "Beatsy? Yeah, 'e's 'ere all readeh."

Jim followed the man down the west wing hallway. The floor was glass and lit a pale green. Each time he stepped on it the area around his foot bloomed purple, only to disappeared when he took his foot away. He heard shouts, screams of laugher, feet running across floors from behind the doors he passed. One was open – a man dressed like MaX Fist was lying on the floor, his head tilted back. Standing over him was a girl dressed as LinX, the romantic lead MaX always had to rescue. She was pissing in his mouth as he cried – to be punished or forgiven, Jim wasn't sure.

"Just another of Jacob's mad parties, man… Through here." The tall man laughed and opened a door.

White leather covered the walls and floor. Lamps lit the room in a low, beige light. Over the music Jim heard talking and laughter. The wall on the far side of the room was made of glass and looked out onto the blazing fire and stage. In front of the window was a sunken seating area. Smoke was rising up in two individual streaks from opposite ends. Jim peered down and saw Jacob and Beatsy looking up at him with smudged smiles and blasted eyes.

Great, Jim thought; Beatsy's mashed.

"Hi, Jacob," Jim said with a big smile.

"You know this man is a genius? It's a bloody brilliant idea for a game. Let me tell you, hands down, for real – he got shot! He actually got shot, man. Gangster! This game could be fuckin' gold dust."

Jim grinned and shrugged like it was an obvious conclusion.

"Why didn't you tell me it was Beatsy who wanted to see me, man! He was the *man* back in the day. The Krayzz man! Graffiti artist *and* DJ! He's a ledge, man!"

"We were talking about business, Jim. 'Ghetto Life'," Beatsy said with the forced precision used only by stoned people.

Jim zeroed in on Beatsy's huge spliff.

"About business, eh, Beats?"

Beatsy slowly pushed himself up and coughed into his hand. He scratched the back of his head, glared back up at Jim and then smiled.

"Yeah, straight and narrow these days. Only business, eh, Jake?"

"Yeah! He, he, he." Jacob's laugh ended in a gurgling cough.

"Well, it looks like you two are getting on fine – you don't need me; I know nothing about computer games."

"This is the genius, let me tell you. What a crib! The big dog here. This guy's got it all." Beatsy said through a wide grin.

"What time do you want me to go on stage tonight, Jacob?" Jim said.

Jacob sucked loudly from a carton of Ribena, then crumpled it up with his fat hand and threw it over his shoulder.

"I want 'Snitches' exploding into the new Millennium. On the strike of twelve, you get me!"

Jacob tried to stand but fell back on the seat, dropping his spliff on the carpet in the process. "Oops! Ha, ha, ha!" He patted his hand around the floor, trying to find it.

"Okay… I'd better go and get ready. Beats?" Jim said, looking worryingly at Beatsy.

Beatsy seemed a little uneasy, as he watched Jacob scrabbling around, looking for the roach end of a spliff in the deep, magnolia shag-pile carpet.

"Beatsy?" Jim said a little louder. "What time you meeting up with Phaser and the crew?"

"Yeah, I said, like, half eleven, man. He wants me to go on stage with 'em, but I'm not sure."

Jacob's head shot up. "He should, don't you think, Jim? The Krayzz back together? Hey! What a night if he did... You back from the dead, then The Krayzz back together! I make things happen! That's what I fuckin' do, man." He slapped the floor in triumph then let out a child-like squeal. "Shit! I found that joint, lads... fuck." He looked at his burnt hand.

"Yeah, sounds like a great idea..." Jim said, walking backwards. "You may want some ice to cool that down, Jacob. Laters." He waved and made his way out.

The tall man had been waiting outside the door and now he led Jim back along the corridor, down the stairs and into the hall.

"You're a fooking legend, man. What a life, man. Living the fookin' dream. If only I had your life, man. You have a top night, our kid."

"I'll try..." Jim smiled and walked out onto the driveway to the sound of drum and bass echoing around the grounds. The smell of bonfires and weed was in the air. Now a thick stream of people was flowing in from the wood over to the stage. Funky dreads, new age travellers, black and white kids in hip-hop clothes. Groups of men and girls in luminous cyber-raver gear. Indie boys with shaggy mod cuts and skinny blue jeans. Girls with white-hot bobbed hair and Mary Quant dresses. Wiry blokes with shaved heads in Fred Perrys, earrings and baggy, low-slung jeans. A jumble sale of kids, a meeting of the tribes from the last century all brought together by Jacob and his reputation. All chugging on Stellas, swigging bottles of wine, offering around litres of cider and spliffs.

Then, amongst the crowd, Jim saw a face he recognised. The face looked back. "Hey, Jim!"

Jim turned his head, but it was too late. Dennis ran over and planted a slap on his shoulder.

"Thanks for bring Dimpy down the other night. Top bloke like, top bloke. I gave 'im my CD. And what did I say? Everyone loves The Den. He's only fuckin' signed me up! You left at the right time, man – told me he's dumping The Tyrants 'cause no one cares now you're not in 'um."

"And now Dimpy has signed *you* up?"

Jim heard sarcastic laughter coming from the procession. Joshi and the other lads from The Railway Hotel were pushing the backs of two mod lads with Small Faces-style haircuts.

"Yeah, mate. Next stop *Top of the Pops!*" said Dennis, slapping Jim's shoulder again.

Jim had no doubt that Dennis would survive the scams and the backstabbing he'd experienced in the music industry. They were nothing compared to what Dennis had been through. Dennis would wear anything, say anything and would not question why. He was a karaoke singer. He wouldn't fight for his songs, for his words; he didn't have any, didn't want them. He just wanted to be famous. He was everything Dimpy needed.

"What are you doing here?" said Jim.

"Getting fucked up, like, with the lads. Forget the past, move on, man, to another millennium – when I take over the world! I heard a rumour that you'd be here singing 'Snitches' tonight. You singing it or wah?" Dennis said, chewing gum, his face bright with anticipation.

"Yeah, I'm singing."

That rush of stage fright – fear, anxiety, whatever people called it – shook Jim's insides from his legs up to the back of his head.

Then he heard a girl scream.

Joshi had become involved in an argument and was now pinning one of the mod lads to the ground as his girlfriend hit Joshi over the head with a bag of beer cans.

"I better sort that animal out. He's going to be my bodyguard on tour …" Dennis grinned. He ran off, then turned back and shouted, "Sorry about the nose… Thanks, man, seriously."

Jim gave him a short nod.

He flipped up the collar of his leather jacket and was starting towards the stage when he felt a tap on his shoulder. A girl with a Joey Ramone-style haircut, biker jacket and miniskirt was staring at him with rabbit-in-the-headlights eyes and a gawping smile.

"Oh. My. God."

Wendy Turner – the girl who had set up the fan club and the 'Where is Jimmy Tyrant?' website. Her chin was trembling.

"Yeah! We love you! We love you, Jim." She turned to a group of indie kids a few feet behind her. "It is him! I knew it!"

The kids looked around, then rushed over.

"Are you singing 'Snitches' tonight, Jim?" one of the lads shouted.

"Yeah. I'd get down the front around midnight if you want a good view." Jim said.

They all cheered. He saw something almost feverish in their expressions of excitement.

"Hey, Jim – look!"

Wendy Turner pulled down her black T-shirt to reveal a plump, milky-white breast with Jim's face tattooed above the nipple. Over his head were the words *The 27 Club*, and underneath, his date of birth and the date he had gone missing.

The group of kids grew closer to him and Wendy. Jim suddenly felt trapped. Dread rose from the pit of his stomach. He smiled and pushed his way past them. "Sorry. Really, sorry. I've got to get back and sound check." His voice went shaky on the last part.

"Hey, we just want to talk…" a boy said.

Jim carried on walking.

"Jim! We thought you were fuckin' dead!" Wendy shouted.

A volley of voices shouted song requests.

"We just want to talk to you! Do you know what you put us through? I'll have to change my tattoo now!"

He checked the time on his phone: it was eleven twenty. He thought he heard a girl shout, "Wanker!", but he carried on across the field, passing dancers and stragglers on the edge of the crowd. Backstage a few cars and transit vans were parked at angles with their doors open and headlights on. A black Cavalier pounded the air with bass notes from sub-woofers in the open boot. Cheeks was talking to a group of hip-hop kids. Taller than all of them by a good foot, he bobbed gently along to the music. Plumes of smoke hung over them like cauliflower bulbs.

Phaser stood next to Cheeks; his voice louder than the others, stressing every word of his story by patting his chest and throwing his hands up, then pointing his finger in one of the crew's faces.

Jim unzipped his jacket and pulled out a small bottle of JD. He took a deep glug and felt instantly that he was going need a lot more, but he stopped. He thought of Lulu and screwed the top back on and put the bottle back in his pocket.

Around the back of the cars he found a white marquee. *Artists* was scrawled in black felt-tip pen across a cardboard label hanging over the doorway. He could have done with another gulp of whisky, but instead he took a deep breath and walked in. Inside it was loud and full of musicians from local bands, DJ collectives and hangers-on. In a cordoned-off area around the stage entrance a collection of tattooed roadies tuned up guitars.

Sizzle was flicking through his records on a red velvet sofa by a table stacked with crates of beer.

"You ready to take 'um into a new century?" said Jim.

Sizzle looked up. "Hey, Jimmy fuckin' Tyrant." Sizzle hand-grabbed Jim and patted his back. "I knew I recognised you before, man! I knew it! Then I saw you on telly."

Jim nodded quickly. "You spoke to Jacob? You know what we're doing?"

"I go on and play a few tunes to get them going. Introduce you, and then we start up 'Snitches', so that when it builds you come in singing the first verse… Listen, about before – it's a great tune, man. Massive in Ibiza, as well as Faliraki."

"Thanks…"

Jim looked around. Most of the people from the other groups – The Backdoors, Hoodoos, The Mirrors with their new singer – were bands he'd been on the same bill with. But unlike him, they'd never got signed. They were looking over and talking in each other's ears, shaking their heads and then turning their backs.

"Sizz, you heard of the phrase 'Crabs in a barrel'?"

Sizzle glanced over at the crowd and nodded. "I get ya. You nervous or sumfin'?"

"I haven't sung for a long time, man. A fuckin' long time…"

Sizzle dropped his hand on Jim's shoulder, looked him in the eye and smiled. "I've seen your videos, man. You've got it. They're all waiting for you. Jimmy Tyrant. You could sing the fuckin' phone book and they'd be happy. They just want Jimmy; you just got to give them Jimmy… Okay?"

Jim nodded.

Sizzle winked, picked up his record box and started walking. Jim followed him, pushing his way through the growing crowd, and walked up a set of steps, through an opening and onto the side of the stage. The Venga Boys' 'We're Going to Ibiza' began playing and the crowd started to boo. A small, round-faced girl, mic headset over her black bob, scurried towards them. Her big Lemur eyes seemed worried.

"They're baying for blood… You ready to go on? What's this shit he's playing? *What is this shit?*" She winced, then turned and shouted down her mic: "We're pulling this loser. Give him the chop, Gaz – get this joker off… You ready, Sizz?"

"Born ready!"

Sizzle ran across to the decks, took out a record, slipped it on and faded 'Going to Ibiza' into 'Praise You' by Fat Boy Slim. The crowd threw up a huge roar and the girl looked at Jim and closed her eyes in relief.

"They're a tough crowd. They're expecting something life-altering tonight. You'd better deliver, Jim."

She walked away and disappeared into the dark space behind the back wall of the stage. She reappeared in the light on the opposite side of the stage, next to the sound desk.

Jim checked his phone. It was ten to twelve.

He looked out at the audience. Arms pumping up and down like pistons to the beat. The sound of whistles being blown rising up with a cloud of steam over the dancers as they twirled and undulated beneath the cold night's stars. The crowd appeared to him like some starved, multi-limbed beast begging to be fed.

He stepped away from the stage and turned to look into the backstage marquee. Phaser and Beatsy had just walked through the entrance. Phaser was grinning and patting Beatsy on the back. They were followed by a group of ten men – the rest of The Krayzz, Jim suspected. They pushed through the gathered musicians with hard faces and a cocky ease, towards the stage.

Then, just behind The Krayzz, Sergeant Doyle entered. She had her hair in bunches and was decked out in day-glo cyber-raver gear. She was followed by Green and four other officers dressed as new age-ravers.

Jim sank the jagged nail of his index finger into the back of his hand and walked away from the door into the darkness behind the stage. Just before he reached the light on the other side he saw a set of steps that led down to the car park where he'd seen Cheeks standing with The Krayzz. He could run down those steps, over the fields and be on his way to Finland within an hour.

Jim had reached the top of the steps when he felt a jab in his arm. He spun around and was faced with Dennis's large, square-toothed smile.

"Nervous, mate? Just pee into this if yer desperate…"

With a genuine look of concern, Dennis held a boozy smelling plastic pint glass under Jim's nose.

"No, ha! No, man! Me, nervous? Walk in the fuckin' park, man. What you doin' here?" Jim said.

"My mate's doing the sound. I got him the mixing desk, like. He gets me the best seat in the house!"

Jim looked out to the mass of flesh and hair jumping in unison, pounding the field, making the stage shake beneath his feet.

"A good view, right…" Jim said

Dennis was staring across to the other side of the stage. Jim looked over to see Phaser walking up from the marquee into the wings. Beatsy followed and stood next to him in the spinning blue-and-red lights. Then the rest of The Krayzz appeared.

Dennis drew in a deep breath and shook his head.

"Dennis?" Jim said and put his hand on Dennis's tense shoulder. "Dennis, not now, mate. Not tonight…"

The song was fading. The crowd began chanting. "Jimmy, Jimmy, Jimmy!"

Jim felt the soft grip of a hand on his arm and saw the girl with the headset at his side.

She smiled. "You ready, Mr Vale? The crowd are waiting for you…"

Sizzle started to spin his remix of 'Snitches'. A roar went up from the crowd, rattling Jim's ear drums.

"Dennis, I wouldn't go over – not now, man. Hey, what about singing backing vocals with me?"

Dennis pushed Jim away, reached into his back pocket and disappeared into the shadow cast by the stage wall, towards Phaser. Jim knew now that it wasn't Beatsy or Burt who had supplied Dennis's sister with the heroin that had killed her. Dennis had known all along that it was Phaser.

The chant of "Jimmy, Jimmy, Jimmy" got louder, more aggressive.

"I'd go on *now* if I were you, Jim."

Jim turned to see DI Craven – in jeans and a day-glo hoodie standing at the top of the steps, three men behind him. He nodded.

"Now, Jim!"

The girl with the headset pulled him away from Craven and before he could squirm free he was out on the stage.

A huge cheer went up. Whistles jack-knifed the air and gas-powered horns sounded.

With each step to the mic he felt as if every atom in his foot had been replaced by lead shot. A waft of cold wind blew cannabis smoke in his face. He looked over at Sizzle, then threw both hands up in the air and leant into his microphone.

"Back from the dead! My good friend. It's Jimmy Tyrant!"

The beat slammed down and Sizzle ramped up the volume.

The crowd pushed forwards, down to the front of the stage.

The volume of the song and the crowds cheers acted like

a power surge blowing out every fibre of his body. He stood shaking, unable to break free of its authority, watching a sea of heads bobbing between outstretched hands that leant like exotic plants towards the source of light from the stage.

Jim nodded to the crowd.

A huge cheer went up.

His left leg began to shake. He put his foot on the mic stand.

Another cheer.

A busted orchestra of whistles and horns.

Jim turned to see what was happening with Dennis and Phaser, but all he saw were faint apparitions swirling in the dark.

He swung his head round. With no hair to shield him from the crowd, he closed his eyes again.

Voices shouted from crushed bodies in the front row:

"Sing the fucking song!"

"Get on with it!"

The beat looped and anticipation pulled heavily inside him. He opened his eyes, head bobbing to the beat.

Another surge in the crowd; lurching to the left, then forwards under the yellow spotlights… He remembered the night on the hill and the yellow city lights, the stagnant pools of people in the city below him – the world he saw had congealed and begun to break down. But these people in front of him weren't stagnant. They were alive. It was in the crowd's movement and their voices – the music, drink, pills and powders jostling inside, allowing them to be pulled and pushed together as one mass with no fear. All anticipating the minute that had taken one thousand years to get to them and that would leave them in a beat of a song – his song. He could see now what this night meant. It was a banner going up, saying, "It's okay. Let go of the past and welcome the future." He too was swirling around with everyone else, looking to break out, looking to move on without fear.

Jim put his mouth on the mic and spat out the first line: "They tell you one thing and mean another…"

The crowd shouted back every word.

He sang the next two lines with controlled hate and distain. The song's rhythm realigned his heartbeat, making him feel lighter. He was smiling. Ephemeral. Ready to be swept away by the wind, part of the music, to a new beginning.

Then he heard it. Gunfire.

His eyes split open, and he was jolted back onto the stage.

Yells and screams came from the audience as they receded, pushing and brawling their way from the front of the stage.

Jim turned back to see Dennis, teeth bared, running towards him. Behind Dennis, he caught sight of Phaser at the side of the stage, one eye closed, raising a gun, the metal flashing blue in the lights. He recognised the gun, had seen the distinctive shape before – the incident at Jumps where Phaser pistol-whipped the businessman.

The chorus of 'Snitches' kicked in but was unable to mask the awesome crack of the second shot.

Dennis smashed into Jim's side and slammed him down onto the floor.

A glassy ringing sound enveloped Jim's head and faded out to the clobber of feet across the stage floorboards.

There was another shot and the music cut out. Feedback screeched from the PA.

Jim felt Dennis's weight pinning him down and a throb burning behind his eyes, a stabbing pain in his shoulder. He raised his head as far as he could.

All the lights were up now.

Sergeant Doyle, Green, Craven and five other undercover policemen were standing in front of Phaser, pointing their guns, shouting, "Don't move! Don't try it."

"Hands on your heads, now!" Craven shouted.

A muffled calm descended.

Then there was a click, and a blinding white flash in Jim's eyes.

Another flash.

This time he could just make out a camera hanging over his face.

"Hey! What the hell do you think you're doing! Get out of here." Sergeant Doyle shouted from the back of the stage.

"Is he dead? Jim, it's Craig, Craig Beakington? Can you hear me?"

"Move or you're going in the back of the van with the others… Now!"

Sergeant Doyle stood towering over Jim.

"I just need to know if he is dead or not," Craig said with the intonation of a spoilt child.

"Leave now!"

Dennis groaned and slid off Jim, onto his side.

Sergeant Doyle's face was close to Jim's now, inspecting his eyes and then his chest.

"Jim can you hear me? Are you hurt?"

Jim patted his shoulder and looked at his hand.

"I'm covered in blood…"

"It's mine, you soft bastard. They shot my fuckin' arm, man. *My* fuckin' arm…" Dennis said, his voice strained and high. He lay motionless on his side.

"What's happened…" Jim said, sitting up.

The stage was fully lit and police officers on loud hailers were directing the crowd to make their way to the exits. He could see Sizzle, still behind his decks, being questioned by a cyber-raver-clad cop.

"Beatsy was just about to receive a bag of cocaine from Phaser so that we could shop him when this doughnut rushes in and tries to floor Phaser with a spanner. Phaser pulls a gun. So we all pull our guns. Green got one in the chest. Laughing boy here runs away and gets shot and then one of the lads brings Phaser down with one in the leg."

"Green's dead?"

"No, just a bit winded. The guns they use are cheap and hardly dented his vest. And that idiot just then was a journalist trying to take your picture. The first one of you dead, no doubt… You did well, pet."

"Thanks for pushing me out the way and saving me like that, Dennis. Thank you."

"I wasn't trying to save you, you daft cunt. I was running away because Phaser was going to shoot me 'cause I came at him with a spanner." With an agonised huff, Dennis flopped onto his back. "So you were in on all this, Jim?" he said and tried to sit up, only to let out a weak, pain-filled cry.

"Just sit back down, er... what's your name?" Sergeant Doyle said.

"Dennis," he said quickly through a sharp intake of breath.

"Okay. You're Dennis Whittle. Sit back and wait for first aid, please. They'll fix you up real soon."

"If it's any consolation, Jim you had the crowd eating out the palm of your hand for a moment there. Took them to another place," Sergeant Doyle said, smiling. "Shame it was cut short."

Jim went to stand. Sergeant Doyle grabbed his forearm and helped him up as DI Craven walked over.

"Better take yourself to get checked out by the paramedics, eh?"

"I'm okay. Really, I'm fine. Inspector, can I have a word with you?"

Craven drew in a big breath and looked down to the riot vans in front of the stage being filled with handcuffed gang members.

"I pretty busy at the moment, Jim. Can it wait?"

"I think you'll thank me, and start buying all my records, with what I've got to tell you."

Craven looked at Jim, unable not to stop himself smiling at such an audacious statement. "Okay. Make it quick..."

After he told him, Craven nodded and said, "We have no other evidence to support this Jim... After what's gone on tonight..."

"I'm just so sure about this, Inspector."

"If that's the case... Go now, but I suspect that he's already fled the sinking ship..."

The doors to the main house were wide open. The music was still pounding, but as Jim made his way up the stairs and along the corridor he could see that all of the rooms were empty.

When he reached Jacob's bedroom he pushed open the

door. A stream of blue smoke was rising from the sunken seats. Jacob was slumped on a sofa with a clear view of the stage and the fields – the wall-length window like a huge TV screen. A cigar-shaped spliff was burning down in a square marble ashtray.

Jacob looked up at Jim with heavy-lidded eyes.

"Get a good view, did you?" Jim said.

"The best view…" Jacob sniggered and turned back to the police vans and ever-dwindling crowd.

Jim sat down next to Jacob. Without the cap Jacob's thinning hair at the crown was visible. His face was a dishwater grey and his stomach touched the top of his legs. He looked more like forty than twenty.

"What were you thinking, Jacob?"

"Just wanted people to have a good time. Give them something they've never seen before."

"You're not stupid and neither am I. You know what I'm talking about, don't you?"

Jacob said nothing for a moment. His lips parted slightly; they looked dry and cracked. Then, quietly, he said, "I was just helping out my friends, blood. I make things happen...." His eyes closed. "Phaser said he needed some help… so I helped him."

"You knew what he was up to, though? You knew he was selling drugs?"

"It was just money, my friend. Said he needed some money and I gave it to him, but I wanted a cut. A silent partner." Jacob opened his eyes now and began to push himself up.

"So this was your next project? A real-life gangster game. Use real people instead of pixels? You can't manipulate real people like characters, Jacob. Real people die. Real people have complicated feelings and reasons for what they do, and they can fight back. Funding a gang's not about improving your fucking score on the last game."

"Oh, you can, James. You most defiantly can manipulate people. You of all people should know about being manipulated. If someone wants something and you have it, you can make them do anything for it."

Jacob stood, swaying a little. He sniggered again and looked out to the last stragglers. "I had Beatsy's idea for a game about gang life way before he did. Way before… By giving money to Phaser I just made 'Ghetto Life' happen in the real world."

"You wanted to take over the dope flow into the city? Be the big man?"

"No. Phaser did. And not just dope. Pills, meds…"

"Meds?"

"Prescription medication. 'Mother's little helper' they used to call it – everyday painkillers for everyday pains."

"Did you make a pill called Co-cocadin?"

Jacob looked at Jim and grinned. "That's our biggest seller – like a notch down from morphine. Strong shit, blood. It was so popular, even your old friend Burt was getting in on the act. I heard he bought a shitload of lab equipment so he could make up a batch. Fucking idiot wouldn't have a fucking clue where to start."

Jim raked the burn on the back of his right hand, let the pain take over the urge to hit Jacob with the nearest blunt object.

"Police told me he was making crack," Jim said.

"What the fuck do they know? Burt was just trying to copy me. As always."

"Is that why you had him killed?"

"No. No. No. Phaser shot him. Not me… He was taking Phaser's business."

"Alright. I get it. You dish out orders and get all the cash, without any involvement."

"As I told you when I saw you last, I manipulate reality," Jacob said proudly.

"Like your shrink said, you're trying to turn the real world into the one you created and gave away."

"You got it, Jimmy boy…" He picked up the spliff and relit it. "How the fuck did you know anyway? Phaser would never squeal, or Beatsy for that matter."

"I wouldn't be so sure of that Jacob."

Jacob Little waved a limp hand that seemed to belittle all that had been said; a gesture that suggested he was beyond care

184

or reproach.

"I found out for myself. Phaser's gun was the same one he cracked off a businessman's nose in Jumps. It was the gun he just pointed at me on stage and shot Dennis Whittle with. It was also the big square gun you pulled on me the first time we met when I dropped off that gear from Burt. It was a replica of MaX Fist's gun. No one would have a gun as ridiculous as that other than you. And you gave it to Phaser, the leader of your favourite hip-hop act, all because you wanted to be the Mac daddy."

Jacob's face grew dark. He dropped his smile and came over to Jim, standing inches from his nose and poking a finger into his chest.

"And what about you? Aren't you doing exactly the same thing? Selling drugs because it's an easy way out?"

Jim pushed him away. Jacob lunged backwards and fell onto the sofa.

"You're not selling to hookers. To single mums. Wasting years worrying that regular customers will fuck off to another dealer for a better price. I admit that what I did was wrong. I've paid the price. Heavily. I bet you never thought that you'd be found out, did you?"

"Look. I'm sure we can talk about this like grownups. How are you fixed at the moment. Got a record deal?"

Jim sniffed and looked away. Jacob tried to focus on Jim. His face contorted into a look of pity and then anger.

The sound of the music buffed against the window. A couple of police sirens cut through.

"Do you realise how bored I was... how boring my fucking life has always been? Since I was a kid all I did was stay in my room, by myself, and write computer programs. I wanted to get out of the world of programming and codes. I wanted to be part of The Krayzz world. No one fucking messes with them, blood. No one! I knew I could never be MaX Fist, but The Krayzz... Doesn't everyone really want to be a gangster? Doesn't everyone want to be listened to and given respect when they ask for it?"

The clatter of heavy-booted feet sounded from the hall and

then the deeper boom of them on the stairs as they got closer to the room.

"I tried to be someone else too... but you're always left with the same body, the same shit that fucked you up in the first place."

Jacob puckered his mouth like he'd sucked a lemon. "How fucking lovely... and neat and fucking sweet. How clever and insightful you are, Jim. But where does it say that there's nothing wrong with trying?"

Jim could smell the hippy whiff of patchouli oil. Craven was standing in doorway with a line of undercover policemen behind him.

"I think you've missed the point, Jacob. You've completely missed the point."

Chapter 22

After being held at the station all night, filling out forms and answering questions about any other drug-related actives he'd witnessed at the party, Jim told Craven and Green about his concerns for Nina. Green told him they would look into it. Because she may be an illegal, tracking her down could prove to be a real problem. She didn't exist on record. They would do their best.

He was given a white T-shirt, a pair of officers' trousers and a high-viz police coat to replace the bloody one. Green explained that Dennis was in a stable condition at the Queen Elizabeth Hospital. The wound was significant and he'd lost a fair amount of blood, but he was being monitored and seemed to be doing well. Beatsy was being debriefed and Phaser was being questioned. They would be contacting him in the next week or so to tie up any loose ends.

"There's a load of press out there, Jim. You ready?" Craven said with ironic concern.

"Just about. One thing, though. Can you call me James Vale?"

Jim walked with Craven down the corridor and out onto the steps of the station in front of a wall of exploding lights, TV cameras and journalists shouting Jim's name. Craven stood next to Jim, cleared his throat at the microphone that had been set up, and the noise cut out.

"I'd like to announce that, as of last night, we've found and arrested the killer of Marion Baines. Raymond Carter, known as Phaser and head of a gang called The Krayzz, was brought in for questioning just after midnight. Mr Carter is also helping with investigations concerning the drugs ring that has been supplying his gang and others with vast quantities of cocaine to distribute within the city. We are also questioning Mr Jacob

Little with regards to his role in the infrastructure."

Craven paused. A volley of questions and flashes exploded once again. Ignoring them, he carried on.

"I would also like to thank James Vale here for helping us significantly in our endeavours to find the killer, putting his own life at risk in the process."

Jim smiled, dropped his head and allowed himself for the first time to feel vindicated. He imagined that he may feel more heroic, but he just felt like he'd done the right thing.

Craig Beakington had slipped to front of the scrum.

"Congratulations, Jim, on the number one spot. Now you're back, we want to know why you vanished in the first place. Is it true what people say, that it was all just a publicity stunt?"

A chaotic jumble of questions followed. Jim started to speak and the questions stopped. "I was confused. Frightened, I suppose. I couldn't be Jimmy Tyrant any more... I needed to figure a few things out."

"So what happened to Jimmy Tyrant? Where is he now?"

The crowd of journalists began to laugh. A blub flashed, whiting out his vision. Nina's twisted arms flashed before his eyes. Then her bloody mouth.

"People go missing every day. I'd like to ask why you don't hold press conferences for those people?"

Jim felt the grip of Craven's wide hand on his shoulder slowly tighten. "Enough of the politics, James," he whispered in Jim's ear.

Then he turned, smiling, to the press.

"James has been a great help to us and I hope that you'll leave him in peace while he recovers from this dreadful event."

Craven's balled fist was pushing against Jim's lower back as he walked him to a police car. Before he got in, Craven leant down and said to Jim, "I think you should know that it was Lawrence Highsmith who was bringing the coke into the city."

They were suddenly surrounded by cameras. Craven pushed Jim's head down into the car and slammed the door. The car sped off.

Jim turned to see the pack of press envelope Craven.

He sat back in the seat, exhausted. The young officer who was driving said nothing, just glanced in the rear-view mirror every other second as if to check that he was real. Jim closed his eyes. The car rolled on down empty roads and Jim let the weak sunlight flick over his eyelids. He went to scratch the sore on the back of his hand, and then stopped, realising that he didn't need to; it wasn't actually itching.

*

Jim filled up the tank of Burt's Escort and headed down the Hagley Road and out onto the Quinton Expressway. Christmas songs by Slade, Wizard and Cliff dominated every channel on the radio. He turned it off and spent the rest of the journey counting the Christmas trees in the windows of houses.

He stopped off at a garage and bought a small yucca plant and a box of Christmas Edition Milk Tray chocolates. He carried on driving, past houses draped in fairy lights, hanging like giant, tarnished jewels from their windows. Father Christmas and his sleigh flashed blue and white on the roof of a bungalow against the blank morning sky.

The halfway house was a red-brick office block off Dudley High Street. The reception smelt like disinfectant and looked like a ward of a hospital, with its strip lights and white lino floor. Though he'd never seen security guards at the doors of a hospital.

The receptionist was a heavy-set, softly spoken woman with plump lips, a snub nose and straw-yellow hair. He asked to see Margaret Vale and filled out a visitor's form, then she led him to his mum's room.

When he walked in his mother was sitting on the side of the bed folding a powder-blue handkerchief into a small square. She didn't look up.

Her hair had been cut since the photo in the *Weekly Music Express.* It was now in a bob and the same colour as Viv's. She was also wearing make-up; a little pink lipstick, black eyeliner. The short sleeves of her blouse showed red, raised scratches across her forearms.

"Merry Christmas," he said, standing with the chocolates against his leg and the yucca plant held out towards her.

Her washed-out blue eyes met his. She considered him with a face that held both weariness and muted affection.

"Do you want to sit down?" she said quietly, looking back at the handkerchief.

Jim sat on a red plastic chair at a table next to the window. He placed the plant on the table along with the Milk Tray.

"Viv said you came to see us the other day?" she said.

"Yes..."

She looked up.

"And your face. What's that?" She pointed to his nose.

"It's nothing that won't heal... How are you feeling?"

"Sober, I suppose. I feel sober. Not my best Christmas..."

She unfolded the handkerchief and smoothed it out on the bed.

"And your leg?"

She glanced down at her neatly bandaged ankle, then spoke to the window.

"Getting there. I'm off the pills I used to take and on some other ones they've given me... Group meetings in the morning. I wanted to go out in the afternoons but they said it was too early for that yet. I asked for a nice piece of fillet steak the other day and the woman just laughed at me. Bloody rude..."

"So when will you be coming out?"

"They say I've got twenty days left here ..." She unfolded the handkerchief again and sniffed.

Jim looked out of the window. He could see to the edge of the town, the countryside. Over the hills on the horizon was Hamblington.

"Since you disappeared we had all sorts coming around, you know" she said. "Mostly girls wanting to see your room. And a few boys." She tutted. "Asking for your clothes, your bed sheets. One girl asked if she could have a pair of your pants. I mean, God's sake… And journalists. Loads of questions about you. So many questions about you…"

He thought for a moment that he saw a smile emerge at the corner of her mouth. She folded the handkerchief again and patted it down to make the edges tidy.

"What did they want to know?" He was worried she may have told them that he used to piss the bed until he was seventeen. "You didn't show them my room, did you?"

"They offered Viv a lot of money –"

"Please say she didn't show people around."

"No, she didn't. I didn't want their mucky footprints on the stairs. Well, at least until I left, she didn't. I wouldn't know if she has done now. Craig offered a lot of money…"

Jim kept his head down. "I'd suggested you get help years ago, Mum. But you wouldn't listen. You never listened to me. You would only listed to Viv."

He felt that ache in his stomach again, like when Viv would talk over him as if he hadn't said anything, like he wasn't even there.

"I suppose so." Margret Vale's face looked confused. "I didn't really listen to Viv that much."

Jim ran a hand over his head. His eyes felt hot and they began to sting. "So you took it? You took the cash?"

"Yes. 'Course we did. You can't blame us, can you. Those bloody press people knocking, shouting day and night." Irritation bubbled up in her voice. "Least I could do was get a couple of quid out of them. Neither of us were working. Viv's back's still playing her up…"

He had wondered what she'd done with the ten grand he had sent her when 'Snitches' went to number one. But looking at her now, in her room at the halfway house, it was obvious where it had gone.

"You know, Jim, I was only doing the best I could. I just… I couldn't cope with everything that had happened. Him leaving then… there just seemed to be too much noise in my head. So much noise going on. It felt better saying nothing. Just being quiet."

The handkerchief; it came back to him – it was his

comforter, the rag he clung to when he was small, when his dad left. And he'd clung to it again when his dad had died from drinking and smoking too much, blotting out the truth; that his chain of amusement arcades had been swallowed by the recession.

"That's why I'm here, Mum. I just want to make things right. Make them like they used to be before…"

Margret Vale's eyes closed slowly and she stopped folding the handkerchief. "Jamie. I know, and you do too, that will never happen, son…" She smiled softly at him and then frowned, looking down at her red, gleaming fingernails.

On her bedside there was a black and white picture of his mum and dad in a thin pine frame. His mum's hair was down to her waist, her small body wrapped tightly against his dad's broad chest, her face bright with a wide smile. His dad's head rested on top of hers – mouth grinning, his thick black fringe falling over his eyes and ears. With his free hand he held the top of a battered acoustic guitar against his leg. Two people in ignorant bliss of the future. Jim must have been around the same age as his dad in the picture. If he'd stood next to him back then, and if it wasn't for his short hair, Jim thought, they would have passed for twin brothers.

"I'd really like it if we talked more, Mum, from now on. If you'd let me help you…" Jim said.

"That's what we're doing, isn't it?" she said, looking directly at him now.

The light and movement that had once been in her eyes had left. He knew she would never get back to being the woman who danced around the room like a pony on its hind legs to the 'Blue Danube', singing along in a strained falsetto to entertain him on wet holiday afternoons. The woman who cried when he sung 'In the Bleak Midwinter' at the dinner table one Christmas Day when he was seven, then laughed, wiping away tears as the family all applauded.

All of that mattered, but not now. He could not bring back these times or his father.

What was important now was the way she looked: her hair, her make-up. Something had changed. She was trying again. He knew this wouldn't have happened a year ago. And displaying the photo of her together with his dad – she was now willing to recognise that he had actually existed, that he was an important person in her life.

As she started folding his comforter again Jim knew nothing would get resolved today, not like this. But for the first time since he had left her, the silence had been broken.

The door opened and the receptionist popped her head round.

"Sorry to interrupt you, Mr Vale, but it's time for your mum's group meeting."

Jim stood, and his mother looked up at him. She smiled and brought her hand up with his handkerchief folded in a warm, soft square.

Jim looked at it. He took it from her hand and slipped it into his coat pocket. He nodded. His mouth had become dry and he swallowed awkwardly.

"Call me when you get out. Okay? Promise?" he said.

Margret Vale looked down at the bed and smoothed the area where the handkerchief had been. "Okay. I'll call you. Promise."

*

Back at Lulu's parents' house, Jim and Lulu spent two days in bed, bathing together and eating the French cheeses that were left over from Christmas. The rest of the week was spent refining lyrics and driving off the paparazzi and TV crews that knocked on the door.

The papers' opinions of Jim were mixed. The *Daily Mail* and *Telegraph* painted him as a junkie deviant – saying that he only got away with his association to a drug dealer and murderer because he was a pop star. The *Guardian* considered his disappearance somewhat dubious, but held that he was actually quite a good songwriter and really, that was all that mattered. *The Mirror* believed him to be a Robin Hood figure with a guitar and felt that more people should tackle their problems like Jim, by helping the police or taking justice into their own hands.

Gary tried to contact him twice since their meeting at The Railway Hotel, but Jim refused to answer the call. Then Jim found an interview with Gary in *The Sun* in which Gary said that Jim was self-obsessed; that *he* wrote most, if not all, the songs; and that Jim's disappearance was a publicity stunt constructed solely by himself. The reporter then revealed that The Tyrants had been dropped by their manager, their future was uncertain, that Gary chain-smoked throughout the interview and that it wasn't just alcohol that Gary smelt of but "sour desperation".

Jim refused any interviews. Aunt Viv called him to say that she was to contribute to a piece in the *Sunday Mirror* magazine talking about the effect of his father's death on the family and his mother's subsequent slip into alcoholism. With the money she was going to check into a rehabilitation clinic down south.

Then, late one afternoon while Lulu was in the bath, he received a text message from an unknown number. *Hey Jim, or can I still call you Rocco!? I'm in London doing promos for a car company. Handing out flyers. I start next year at collage for Dentists. Thank you for what you did. I will always be grateful. Talia XXXX*

A minute later he received another text: *Hey! I love 'Snitches' BTW. PS Not as much as Barry White tho… ;-)*

Jim grinned and looked at the message for a while. Lulu walked out of the bathroom.

"What's so funny?" she said.

He quickly flipped the cover up on it and placed the phone in his back pocket.

"Oh, nothing, babe. It wasn't anything." He stood up and kissed Lulu's warm, sweet-smelling head. "I'm just happy this whole thing is all over with, that's all."

As they walked up to the departure lounge Jim noticed the headlines on the front pages of the *Birmingham Mirror*: *Rapper Un-Va/ed as Drug Dealer Killer*. He bought the paper and read the article out loud to Lulu as they ate their breakfast in the departure lounge.

"'Raymond Carter, a.k.a. Phaser, the head of the rap collective and drug gang The Krayzz, was sentenced to thirty years for murder and six other drug-related charges at Birmingham Crown Court yesterday.'"

Jim breathed out and carried on.

"'Detective Inspector Craven of the West Mercia Police explained to our paper that after extensive questioning Mr Carter told him about a "big plan" that he had laid out for the future of his gang involving funding from several supposedly "legitimate" sources; one of whom is rumoured to be washed-up teen Internet millionaire Jacob Little. Mr Carter's idea was to eventually control the main flow of drugs to the smaller gangs and become top dog in the city's drug's trade.'"

"Doesn't it scare you to know that's who you were dealing with?" Lulu said.

Jim carried on reading out the article.

"'It has also been disclosed that Phaser's girlfriend'" –Jim raised an eyebrow –" Nina Latova, a dancer at The Jumps Gentlemen's Club, was found badly beaten with a broken arm, jaw and ankle outside a public toilet on Digbeth High Street. She is now in a stable condition at City Hospital. At the moment she is still unable to give evidence, but it is hoped that she can shed more light on the death of Jumps owner Lawrence Highsmith, who was found stabbed to death outside his car the same night.'"

Jim shook his head. "My God, Nina and Phaser were going out with each other. It makes sense now."

"What? I don't get it?" Lulu said.

"Phaser must have known Burt was desperate, that he was owed money by Lawrence and that he'd have done anything for Nina. He probably got her to make up the story about the abortion and Lawrence treating her like shit, so that Burt would feel even more sorry for her. I reckon Phaser was hoping that, along with his money problems, it would drive Burt on to knock Lawrence off, saving Phaser the trouble of doing it himself. Then he could take over Lawrence's business setup. Phaser's problem was that he thought Burt worked like him.

He wasn't able to understand that poor old Burt couldn't kill anyone."

"So why did Nina try to kill Lawrence?"

"Phaser had a hold on her. He was filling her habit. When he found out that Burt wasn't taking the bait, he must have stopped topping her up with coke. Desperate to score, and the fact that she genuinely hated Lawrence for the way he treated her and those girls – she just snapped. It wasn't hard to hate Lawrence –"

A muffled voice announced something about the imminent departure of a flight. Jim looked up at the departure board.

"You said all you had to do that night was sing…" Lulu said.

Jim stood up and grabbed his bag, "If I'd known what was going to happen, Lu, believe me, I wouldn't have gone. But looking back, I needed to prove something…Jimmy Tyrant has truly left the building. Come on, drink up. We've got five minutes to get to the departure gate."

Chapter 23

Walking out through the arrival lounge doors of Oulu airport, the air was crowded with a biting and snowy wind. A red four-by-four pulled up and a shaven-headed man with a yellow, droopy moustache, dressed in an all-in-one-yellow snowsuit, eased himself out of the driver's seat. Without saying a word, he picked up their bags and placed them carefully in the boot. Then, in a deep, croaky voice, he introduced himself as Miki, and opened the back door for them to get in.

Miki drove them in silence down icy roads, through forests where snow cluttered between trees and sprayed the bark of the pines white. Through an opening Jim glimpsed the dull, silver-coloured surface of a frozen lake, a fishing boat halfway out, locked in by the ice.

After another half hour of snow-bleached landscape they pulled off the road onto a driveway and into a wood populated by bony, white trees. Lulu gripped Jim's hand and gave him an excited smile. The car stopped outside three red wooden houses of classic Finnish design. The middle one looked like the main house – large, two floors with pointed bay windows and a turret. The buildings either side were single storey and oblong in shape.

Jim jumped out and felt the cold seep like freezing water through his leather jacket. His eyelashes were already starting to stiffen with the frost.

The front door of the main house opened.

Bix was small and slight of frame with white hair and reminded Jim of a skinnier version of Rutger Hauer in *Blade Runner*. He was wearing a tight black T-shirt, ripped white jeans and large fawn-coloured boots.

"Hey, hey!" he said, his face flushed, steam blowing from his wide mouth. He hugged Jim and looked him up and down. "I saw the papers, Jimmy. Wow, you're a fuckin' hero!" He cupped Jim's face and laughed with his mouth open and head back.

"It depends on your point of view, I suppose," Jim said, looking over at Lulu.

"He's being modest." Lulu smiled, shutting the door of the four-by-four.

Bix flashed a quick, squinty glance at Lulu.

"This is Lulu. She co-wrote the songs."

"Okay…" said Bix airily. Then he looked back at Jim, grabbed his shoulders and turned him towards the door. "It must have been a long journey to get here. Let's get in the warm, hum? Drink some hot chocolate!"

Bix slipped his branch-like arm through Jim's and escorted him into the house. Miki picked up Jim's bag and followed them, leaving Lulu to drag her suitcase across the snowy courtyard.

Bix gave them a brief tour of the studio and showed them to the long and airy kitchen.

After dinner of roasted reindeer, mashed potatoes covered in a cloudberry sauce, Bix burnt incense and talked excitedly over the round wooden table about Jim singing under a large mirrored dome, to get "a really amazing reverb effect. Like in space!" He explained, with all the seriousness of a scientist, that he would like to construct a situation where he may provoke Jim "to achieve an angry response!", to elicit the right vocal take on 'Clandestine'. He spoke with swift arms flailing and countless cigarettes being lit and not smoked.

Jim couldn't believe that Bix Pillar had given so much thought to his music. He was elated by every wacky and seemingly impractical idea that he proposed. But as he went on talking, he realised that Bix never addressed Lulu once. When Jim eventually managed to mention that she had all the piano parts written and ready to go, Bix carried on talking, his eyes bobbing around in their sockets, about how he would like to record 'Ghost Stories' after they had taken some organic weed and tried contacting Jim's father via a Ouija board.

Lulu shuffled in her seat. She coughed and said, "I don't

think it would be appropriate, do you, Jim?"

Bix picked up another cigarette, looked at it briefly and turned to Jim. "So we start tomorrow, after we –"

"Lu's right, Bix. I'm not into the idea of trying to contact my dad. I know where he is… thanks. He won't be answering."

Bix, whose face had been frozen in a look of stunned rectitude since Jim had interrupted, stood and scuffed towards the door with the unlit cigarette bobbing up and down in his mouth.

"Sure, sure…" The tone was softer. "See you in the morning, Jimmy… Miki will take you to your room."

Without looking back at them, Bix pulled the door open and slipped out.

Jim turned to Lulu and gave a meek smile.

"Oh, you do know I exist then?" She looked around the room in mock surprise. "Jesus." She pulled over her vodka and tipped it back.

"Lu, he's an eccentric; he comes up with crazy ideas. This is his creative process. Bix is in his own world. We kind of knew that before we came. Bix is just excitable."

"That, right there, was a major cold shoulder, *Jimmy*." She mimicked his accent. "He just bloody blanked me out completely." She drained the last drop from her glass and fell back in her seat, looking up at the ceiling.

"When we're in the studio tomorrow it'll be a different story. This is Bix Pillar, remember. The man who recorded Nick Cave in a cave…"

She looked crumpled, running both hands tightly over her head and mouthing something to herself so quietly that Jim couldn't hear.

"What's that?" he asked.

"Nothing."

Miki walked Jim and Lulu out to their room. The sky was starless and dark. Jim looked up through the fuzz of fat snowflakes that were now falling slowly around them in the yellow lamplight of the courtyard.

"Hey, Miki, you get the Northern Lights up here?" said Jim.

"Sure."

"Ever seen 'um?"

"Sure."

"Do you think I'll get to see them?"

"They don't always come; you can't always see them. Like a trick of the light. Only lucky ones see them."

Miki said no more. He walked them to the building on the left of the main house, unlocked the front door and opened it.

"This is where we're staying?" said Jim.

Miki nodded, then walked in, followed by Jim and Lulu. The room was small and smelt of sweat and creosote. There was one thin window with black fabric rolled up across the top, to act as a curtain. A double-bed took up most of the space with a single wardrobe on the left. In the opposite corner was a shower with no curtain. Around the taps and base, the grout between the tiles had gone black with mildew.

"Ok. Thanks, Miki..." Jim said.

Miki nodded and left. They stood at the door and watched Miki make his way back across the freshly laid snow and back into the main house.

"So where do we go to the toilet?" Lulu said.

Jim looked back at the shower.

"I don't even want to think about it."

It was still dark when there was a thunderous bang on the door. Jim answered it to find Bix wrapped in a towelling gown and flip-flops, his exposed toes closed in by snow. He was smiling and holding out an identical robe and pair of flip-flops.

"Sowner time."

"Sowner?"

"Yes. Come." He threw the gown at Jim's head.

"What about Lulu? She's fast asleep."

"In sowner? No Lulu. No Lulu... let her sleep. Come!"

The sauna was no more than a dark wooden shed on the snow-covered bank of the frozen lake at the back of the studio. Inside it hummed of secreted human oils and rotting leaves. They sat naked on a pine bench. Bix picked up the wooden ladle from the bucket of water and poured its contents onto the white and grey rocks that lay in a tray next to him. They sizzled as the small room filled with a biting hot steam. For a moment Bix was completely enveloped.

"This is how we start the day… purge ourselves of impurities so we can let good things in."

Jim swallowed a gulp of steam and coughed.

The heat rose and Bix talked more about his most famous collaborations, how he could help sculpt Jim's songs, help "pull inspiration from the air and make magic". After what Jim thought was an hour in the sauna, but what was actually twenty minutes, he felt near to passing out. Bix sprang open the door, ran silently across the snowy bank and plunged through a hole that had been made in the frozen lake. His head disappeared briefly and then bobbed back up.

"Your turn, Jimmy! Wakes you up!" he shouted, his voice taut and shaking with cold.

"Standing naked in the snow is working just about fine for me, Bix!"

Bix scrabbled up the bank and sprang to his feet, looking like a freshly plucked chicken. The cheeks of his tiny arse were pink and puckered.

"Let's make some music, Jimmy. Eh? Now we are clean," he said, slipping into his oversized towelling gown and stomping back to the house.

Back in the bedroom Jim dried himself off and dressed. Lulu didn't stir; he doubted an earthquake could wake her. He felt a surge of warmth rise within him; these emotions were the truest he'd ever had for her, for anyone. She'd given him a second chance. There was a slight uneasy sensation too that sat darkly within him, that this feeling could, so easily, be taken away. He touched the back of his hand to her hair that lay across the pillow, kissed her softly on the cheek and made his way quietly out of the room.

In the studio four tall, squared-headed twenty-somethings in red lumberjack shirts and white denim jeans sat around the room, smoking, laughing and speaking with Bix in deep, impenetrable Finnish voices. Smoke spiralled from an incense stick on the desk.

"Hey, Jim!" one of them shouted. He stood and saluted Jim in a faux-military manner and the others all laughed heartily again. Jim's smile was uneven; he didn't know whether they were taking the piss out of *him* or laughing at this man's mode of address.

"These are your musicians, Jimmy. The Breaknecks. Best in Europe."

"Hi," Jim said.

He nodded at them, but they continued to laugh and talk amongst themselves.

"So, my friend, are you ready to make magic?" Bix said, his serene grin suggesting he was more yogi or spiritual master than record producer.

Then the musician who had saluted Jim suddenly jumped up and landed heavily on one of the others sitting on the long brown-leather sofa. The other two musicians threw up their hands, spitting out Finnish words bound in aggression and mockery, watching the scrap like it was a dog fight.

Jim waited for it to stop. When it didn't, he cleared his throat and spoke loudly. "Guys? I'm going have to get Lulu now. I'll need her to show you the arrangements on the piano, if that's okay?"

The musicians stopped laughing. They all looked over, quick and eager, like prairie dogs, to Bix, who had his feet up on the mixing desk and his arms crossed over his chest. Jim heard the tiny hiss of electrical equipment.

"Er, she won't need to do that, Jim. You can show them the songs on your guitar, that's fine… let her rest."

"No, the thing is that we wrote them together. I wouldn't be here if it wasn't for her arrangements."

Bix wrinkled his forehead and smiled as he drew in air through his nostrils. "No…" He laughed. "No, you don't understand. It will just be me and you. It's one-on-one with Bix. Like I said. It's how I have always worked. I have got the sales to prove it works. That's how I make my art. I chose the band and create furiously, one-on-one."

The musicians on the sofa slowly broke apart from each

other and sat back in their seats.

Jim looked at Bix in silence. Bix smiled back and held his stare for a moment, then gave in.

"You are here, Jim, because of *you*. *You're* the one who got everyone's attention. The star! What you did... you created this, Jimmy Tyrant. You wouldn't be here if you hadn't, understand? If you want to carry on like that, being the star, it needs to be me and you."

"So what do you expect me to tell Lu?"

Bix blurted out a phrase in Finnish and the musicians and Bix erupted into laughter.

"Bix!" Jim shouted. His hand started to burn with an itch and he began working a fingernail on the back of his left hand.

"Hey! Bix! In English, please. Share the fuckin' joke..."

"I said, you tell her to keep her cunt open and her mouth closed!"

They fell about laughing again.

Jim was seized with the urge to cut them all down with a huge sword. He stood frozen, imagining snapping Bix's brittle bones and crushing them in a dusty pile. But he wouldn't stand a chance against the musicians, and the feeling of helplessness that consumed him burnt Bix's sickening phrase even deeper into his heart.

The door swished open and Miki walked in, rubbing his jaw. He knelt down next to Bix and spoke quietly in his ear. The only word Jim understood was "Lulu". Bix's eyes drifted up to Jim and then back to his hands, crossed in his lap.

"Bix, I demand to know what the fuck is going on. Now. This is not what I expected from you. At all."

"Bix only works one-on-one, Jim."

Jim lurched towards Bix, his fists up and clenched.

Bix shot up out of his chair. "Fuck!"

Miki threw up an arm blocking Jim from getting nearer.

"What's happened to Lulu? I heard her name just then, as you were speaking."

Bix shook his head fussily and waved his hand. "Nothing has *happened* to Lulu. Nothing at all. My God, Jim! But you need to tell her she is not to come into the studio. Miki says she is trying to get in. That she punched him. My God! But she is not allowed in. Okay? You have to tell her that… Okay, Jim?"

Behind him he heard grunts and slaps as the play fight broke out again on the sofa.

Jim dropped his arms and moved back from Miki. "Okay, okay, I'll tell her. I'll go now."

Bix put his hands together and raised his eyebrows.

"Good." He smiled slowly. "Now we're getting somewhere."

Jim walked out into the freezing wind blowing across the white courtyard and pushed open the door of their room. Lulu was hunched over, crying, at the end of the bed.

"Come on, put your coat on…"

She looked up with red eyes and wet cheeks. "He told me I couldn't go in. I was to stay in the chalet till you finished for that day… I mean, what the fuck… I swung for him. He's pretty solid. He held me back, stopped me from going in."

Jim grabbed his bag from the floor and threw it on the bed. "Yeah, well, I don't want to go back in." He opened the wardrobe and began to throw his shirts and jeans into the bag.

"What do you mean?"

"I mean I don't want to go back in… with them."

"But Jim, we're here now. Wasn't the whole point for you to get here… to record with Bix?" She dropped her head.

"Don't worry about me."

Jim stopped, sat down next to her and put his arm around her shoulders – she felt too small, bony.

"I came here to record with Bix and with you. We wrote the songs together; that was the whole point, wasn't it? You and me? But that… ego gone mad in there wants it to be me and him. He says it's worked for all the other artists in the past… Maybe it did." Jim tried to focus on Lulu but couldn't; he couldn't focus on anything, speaking only to the room.

"If you ask me honestly? All this 'one-on-one' talk is pure and utter bullshit. It's about the money, babe. He wants half the royalties, that's all. He doesn't care about music or us… And you know what?"

Lulu looked up at him and rubbed away tears with the back of her hand.

"The way it is at the moment, with that sky out there, the clouds covering it, we're not even going to see the Northern Lights."

He stood up. "Come on." He placed his hand gently on her head. "Get packing."

Jim told Bix that he was leaving. Without Lulu, it was a no-go. Bix shrugged and said okay, but he would have to have at least five thousand euro for the band and the mirrored dome he'd hired for the vocal booth. Also, Miki would have to take the band back first, so they would have to wait. The only other option was that Jim could borrow Bix's old four-by-four and then Bix would get someone to pick it up at the airport.

It was a deal.

Bix nodded and told Miki to get the keys. With a mixture of pity and boredom, Bix held up his hand, turned and slinked off without a word, back to the studio.

Miki handed Jim a map and a thermos of coffee through the window and then Jim started the engine, drove out through the forest and onto the lane. As the four-by-four skimmed over patches of black and white road, the snow stopped falling and the sun began to burn away the clouds.

They drove in silence.

Jim had a feeling of awe at what he'd done. He imagined this felt like standing at the base of Everest and looking up to the peak, knowing that a great journey was about to begin. This was the first important decision he had made in his entire life and he felt as if he'd been filled with helium. He glanced over at Lulu; her wide glossy brown eyes shone as she took in their surroundings.

The world around them was blazing with light, the trees flashing silver prisms across the windows. The smell of tobacco and petrol reminded him of his dad's old Triumph and the trips he'd taken as a kid and his thoughts then of "the future". The world that lay before him was so different to the one he'd been in that night on the hill. It smelt different, it tasted different. This was a world he'd fought for and won. Jimmy Tyrant, Robbie Johnson, DJ Rocco were all gone. For the first time being James Vale felt right.

"So what are you going to say to the labels? Now that you've turned down multi-award-winning and platinum-selling Bix Pillar? They'll think you really are fuckin' mad, babe."

He felt a smile open his mouth. "Let them think what they want. I'm twenty-eight in a week's time." Jim took his right hand off the steering wheel and gripped Lulu's slight, mitted hand.

"What about the record?" she said.

"We'll hire a studio. Do it ourselves."

Lulu smiled, but her eyes showed that she still wasn't sure. She went to speak.

"Look, before you say anything, right," Jim said, "I've had this tune looping around my head. It came to me the night on the hill when I was half-dead. For some stupid reason I felt I had to follow it. It was this beautiful and simple tune, and for ages I couldn't tell who was singing it or what instrument was playing it. I just heard this amazing sound that would never leave me. But then, one night, I was lying in the bath at The Railway Hotel and I realised after hearing it over and over that it was obvious. It was your voice that was singing it, Lu. Do you understand what I'm saying? Following it kept me alive. We need to record that tune. Work it out. I just don't know how the hell I'm going to get it out of my head."

Lulu put her hand on Jim's leg, gave it a short, firm squeeze and put a finger to her lips. "Jim…" He'd thrown her from her original thought, he could see. "That's amazing… so, sweet. I can't, well… Don't worry about the tune. Seriously. If it's my song, well, then let me write it?"

"You write it? But how will you know what it sounds like…" He looked over to her and she pursed her lips and gave a reassuring nod.

"Let you write it… Okay. Sure."

"Jim. One more thing. A pretty important thing. We've been driving for hours. How far is it to the airport?"

"I don't know," Jim said with a helpless grin. "I've just been driving. Just going forward… I think we may be lost."

"Seriously?" The smile dropped and she let go of his hand. "You really don't know where we're going, Jim? Really?"

"I haven't got a clue, not a clue…" Jim looked ahead at the bleached landscape that carried on before them. "Don't worry, babe. I've got a map. I'll get us there."

THE END.

Acknowledgements

Thanks:

First and foremost: Liz and Mabel. Mom, Dad and Hayley.

Thanks also go to: Candi Miller, Jackie Gay, Nicola Monahagn, Ian Marchant, Alan Beard, David Savill, Fiona Joseph, Luke Brown, Tindal Street Fiction Group and Charlie Wilson for all your help, encouragement and advice.

Also thanks to Alex Edwards at Andertype for the great art work and thanks to Adam Davis for typesetting.

Lightning Source UK Ltd.
Milton Keynes UK
UKOW030848021212

203006UK00004B/8/P